A Mid-Summer Murder

A Mid-Summer Murder

A Shop 'Round the World Mystery

Geri Krotow

TULE
PUBLISHING

Dedication

For Misha—
I know you found Shadow on the other side.

Chapter One

IS THERE ANYTHING more grounding than the tweet of birds at the dawn of a new day? I don't think so, and neither does Ralph, my one-pound yellow-naped Amazon parrot. We're both sitting on my back balcony—me on the glider bench with Ralph perched on my shoulder—on the third floor of the circa-1820 building I purchased when I moved home to Stonebridge, Pennsylvania. I signed my full name, Angel Strooper Warren, on the deed a little over a year ago.

One year. How can so much have changed in such a short time? I went from Commander Warren, United States Navy, to a retired naval aviator after twenty-two years of active duty. I still fly, but now it's the Cessna that I rent every so often at my local airport, and not the Seahawk helicopter I did hundreds of ship and aircraft carrier landings in.

No longer one of the less than 1 percent of Americans serving on the "tip of the spear," I'm making a go of hometown life and running my own small business.

"Life is very, very good, isn't it, Ralph?" From here we

get a glimpse of the rolling foothills of the Appalachians, but mostly we take in the other buildings and the residential yards that abut the back alley behind my property. Well, I mean *I* get a glimpse. I have no idea how much Ralph takes in, but since his eyesight is exponentially better than mine, I imagine he's spotting hawks that circle high above our valley, invisible to me without my binoculars.

It's full-on summer and this is the coolest it'll be all day. Ralph snuggles into the crook of my neck, lowering his beak to my shoulder and inviting a scratch. As I gently rub under his feathers, a sharp point hits my finger pad. It must be painful where it pokes through his soft, paper-thin skin.

"Aww, poor baby bird, do you have quills coming in?"

He replies with a low birdie murmur, followed by some beak grinding. The sawing together of his upper and lower beak is Ralph's way of letting me know I'm comforting him, that he's content.

I didn't always allow him to sit on my shoulder as that's like telling a parrot they're in charge of your life. When a parrot is eye level with you, as in on a shoulder, their birdie brain tells them they're an equal. Which means they may feel the need to assert their dominance. Ralph's given me a nasty bite here and there, and I have no desire to repierce my ears at the age of…fortyish. Okay, I'm forty-five. Since Ralph basically saved my life last Thanksgiving, I've risked allowing him to use my shoulder like a tree branch.

We've lived a life beyond my imaginings since we've

been back in Stonebridge, including a murder in my international gift shop downstairs. When I made the decision to retire to south central Pennsylvania, I never, ever imagined that small-town life could become so complicated, so fast. Transitioning from being in charge of over five hundred sailors at my last command to becoming the new woman in town who owns the eclectic curio shop seemed manageable. But then there was a murder in my store before it even opened. Which turned me into an investigator of sorts. After I pushed my bestie, the town's senior (only) detective, to let me help.

"Good morning." Ralph nudges me out of my mind's attempt to relive what I've come to think of as the "shock and awe" time. Shock at finding my high school classmate dead, murdered, in my shop no less. Awe at how I found a new talent I didn't realize I had: crime solving.

The Navy taught me a lot of things, gave me skills that translate well to running a business. Turns out the same skill set goes a long way in solving a murder.

That was seven months ago. As my time here increases—along with my regular customers—I'm hoping that we all forget that I once helped to solve a murder. Let's all agree that it's not what I want on my gravestone. Not that I want an epithet of any kind. I want to be cremated with my remains buried at sea. But that's neither here nor there.

The scent of roses from Mrs. Carver's prized garden is heavy in the humid air, and I shift my gaze downward and focus on her little paradise. It's the next street over, kitty-corner from my building, across the tiny alley that runs behind all of the buildings on Main Street.

Downtown Stonebridge isn't unlike any other North American small town. The original section of it is a neat grid of streets, dating back to the early part of the nineteenth century. Some of the Victorian homes added over the following century remain, with many divided into apartments, offices, and more recently, condos. But not Mrs. Carver's place. She keeps her garden lush, and it reminds me of the English manors Tom and I took the girls to when we were stationed overseas.

Tom. I smile at the memory of my deceased husband, grateful that my tears have turned to an acceptance. Tom was taken from us nearly six years ago, gone too soon, thanks to a nasty form of cancer. I'm no longer regularly sobbing, breaking down from the relentless waves of grief that swamped me the first couple of years after he had passed. It's true that time helps, no question. But I think being where I'm loved the most has made all the difference in moving on.

Stonebridge has a been a big part of my healing.

"Yip yippity yip!" Admiral Nelson, the O'Ryans' Chihuahua, has been allowed into the nautical-themed yard that's next to the Carvers' and directly behind me. From my balcony's vantage, I watch as the tiny mammal scurries over to the flagpole and lifts his even tinier leg to nourish Mrs. O'Ryan's fire-engine red and optical-white geraniums. They

were interspersed with tiny blue flowers only a few days ago, but I assume the heat got to them. Or Admiral Nelson's urine.

"Admiral Nelson, you know you're not supposed to pee over there." Mrs. O'Ryan's octogenarian voice drifts up to us, and Ralph ruffles all his feathers at once, sprinkling me with his fine dander. It's as if he's horrified to breathe in the same air as any other creature without feathers.

"Thanks, Ralph. It's okay. You don't own the universe." It's not lost on me that two animals weighing less than five pounds combined can have such oversized personalities. And I'm talking to one of them as if he's a human.

"Come on in now, Admiral Nelson. Daddy has a special treat for you!" Mrs. O'Ryan raises her voice, as if cueing her husband, somewhere inside their home.

A quick suggestion? If you ever are introduced to Admiral Nelson, make sure you don't forget that "Admiral" is as much a part of the doggy's name as "Nelson." Otherwise you'll be listening to Mrs. O'Ryan explain how he's named after her great-great-too-many-to-count-great grandfather Admiral Nelson. Her husband is retired Navy Captain Richard O'Ryan. Captain Rick is a Naval Academy graduate like me, except he attended when the concept of women serving as midshipmen and fleet officers seemed not only a dream but a full-on nightmare. Mrs. O'Ryan has expressed her belief that "war jobs are best left to the men, dear" to me, and I gave her my best "bless your heart" smile. Same with

Captain Rick. We're cordial, but whenever we pass on the street, he peers at me through his frameless lenses as if I'm some kind of insect specimen. A known entity, but not accepted as part of the local environment. I'm okay with our hello, good-bye relationship. For now, anyway. I do hope that someday we'll get a chance to compare career notes and Captain Rick will see that the best values have remained at Annapolis, and all of the changes since he was a midshipman have been beneficial for both the Navy and the nation.

"Admiral Nelson! You get over here!" Mrs. O'Ryan's croaky whisper is louder than some of Ralph's chatter.

"That's our signal, Ralph." Admiral Nelson gets let out at seven a.m. on the dot, right as I finish my first cup of coffee. Time to get dressed and grab some breakfast.

Ralph emits a lengthy cackle that carries over the entire back street. I hate to admit it but it's the exact replica of my laughter. Ralph's vocalization sets Admiral Nelson off into a yipping frenzy, at which Ralph—the quintessential ham— bellows his bomb-falling sound. He learned it from cartoons, honest. I manage to get us back inside and close the balcony door before his high-pitched descending whistle ends with a very punctuated *boom*!

I put Ralph on his cage top and head for the shower, both of us either singing or whistling to music I stream over wireless speakers. My twin daughters, Ava and Lily, are home from college for the summer and have already gone to their other part-time jobs. There's no one to worry about waking up, so I crank the tunes up a bit more and step into the tiled shower that was part of the renovation that transformed the dilapidated building into a showpiece. Water streams from the rainfall shower faucet, and I breathe in the eucalyptus essential oil–scented soap that's part of the Spanish soap collection I have on sale in my shop.

It's a typical start to a summer day in Stonebridge. Except today is Saturday, so I'm going to take off a few hours earlier this afternoon from my international gift store, Shop 'Round the World, and my brother, Bryce, is taking time from Skeins and Baahls, the yarn shop he owns with his husband. Our plan is to have some sibling fun.

We're going tubing, as in floating down our local creek, Jacob's Run, atop our overinflated plastic inflatables. People ride all kinds of floats on the water, but most look like a colorful version of tire inner tubes, when tires had such things. People kayak and canoe on the creek, too, but tubing is unique in that you have to relax and literally go with the flow of the water. The current ranges from a fun clip after a summer storm to barely above a trickle during drought season. Tubing was our favorite pastime as kids.

When I came home, I promised myself to work on my relationships with each of my two siblings. I can't make up for being gone for so long, nor do I feel I need to. Serving my country was the best reason to be away. I can, however, get to know my brother and sister better.

Bryce is two years older than me, and Crystal is two years

older than Bryce. Crystal and her husband, Brad, have built a garden and landscaping business together over the past thirty years. Brad handles all things landscape and hardscape, and Crystal runs the thriving nursery and florist shop.

Crystal and I do lots of girly things together, including the recent spa day we shared at Stonebridge Serenity Spa. Other than knitting and spending time looking over my shop inventory together, it's more difficult for Bryce and me to find fun things to do as a team. I'm looking forward to our creek adventure.

I start to perspire the minute I'm out of the shower. After yesterday's downpour, Jacob's Run should offer a bit of breeze with the faster water. It'll be the perfect respite from the humidity. Even if the flow was its usual snail's crawl, it'd be a reprieve from the constant pace of retail during tourist season. The five-mile-long creek parallels Main Street, but at its closest point of approach, it is over a quarter of a mile from the town center. In addition to the ample grassy, wooded banks on either side, the waterway boasts a hiking trail that is an offshoot of the Appalachian Trail.

Jacob's Run is part of the Conodoguinet system of waterways that eventually spill into the Susquehanna River, which in turn empties into the Chesapeake Bay. It would take years to explore all of the tributaries in our slice of the world. I'll settle for our modest length of creek.

We're no longer tweens. Between our work responsibilities and, let's face it, more, ah, mature—that's it, mature, not old or aging, no way!—bodies, the ability to spend an entire day riding the local waterways is a thing of the past. So we've agreed to grab what we can. As much as I'm looking forward to relaxing on the float, I'm going for an ulterior motive: humor. No one makes me full-on belly laugh like Bryce. Because no one can speak the truth like a brother.

Only a couple of hours of work are between me and my exclusive comedy show, aka my brother, Bryce.

SHOP 'ROUND THE World smells like a sunny beach day, thanks to my signature scent of the month wafting from the candle display. Summer weekends are my favorites because as the day wears on, the brass bells on the entrance door chime incessantly. The customers, many tourists, come in to peruse my wares, often carrying an iced drink from Latte Love. A customer's gasp of delight at a newfound treasure usually leads to the electronic *ding* of a sale.

I'm at my usual place during store hours, behind the custom counter made from reclaimed Pennsylvania barnwood, tapping on the tablet that I had imbedded into an antique cash register. The register's keys were declared DOA after I scavenged it from an estate sale. I get so many compliments on the shop's ambiance, and I credit my military training for it. Not the ambiance, but how I had to pay attention to the tiniest details to make it all come together. It wasn't just making sure I had the right angles, the best merchandising surfaces. True, the custom-built oak shelving and display tables are arranged using feng shui principles I learned over many Navy moves. And the choice of store stock comes from years of digging through open-air markets all over the planet, giving Shop 'Round the World an international flavor not often seen in south central Pennsylvania. It's my belief, however, that the glue that keeps my brand fresh and intact is the constant scrutiny I give each and every nook and cranny of the store. From the original shelving setup down to the exact shades of yellow I chose for the Diwali linens, it is all a deliberate attempt to make the store instantly welcoming, to allow the most sparkly mementos of my travels to shine light into my customers' lives.

The shop is set up by countries and cultures, and I'm quite pleased with the variety of merchandise. Not only in type and items but in the colorful way the displays seem to sprinkle the store with happiness, like the multicolored dots on the outside of a jawbreaker candy.

Bright blues and deep greens dominate the Japanese tea set shelf, deep reds and golds splash across hand-painted Matryoshka nesting dolls from Poland and Russia, and white porcelain from Belgium and Luxembourg balance the center of the space. And those are just the mainstays. I rotate merchandise seasonally, as well. The shelves that hold French cookware in red, white, and blue held hand-painted Polish and Ukrainian Easter eggs only a few months before, and hand-carved Russian Santas only a few months before that.

I look up from the inventory list I'm working on in between customers and see why it's grown quiet. There are only two customers in the shop at the moment. Three, if you count the large chocolate Labrador sniffing the air while his owner stares at the display of essential oils and candles. I wonder what the dog's picking up on. There certainly isn't a dog treat–scented candle in my stock, but I do have a basketful of multicolored dog toys in the "globe-trotting pets" area across the room.

I recognize the woman, as she's one of my best customers to date. Verity Price is constantly in search of unique items for her garden, and I'm constantly in search of high-quality items to meet her desires. She's checking out a Japanese ceramic tea set and matching cast-iron teapot, both in a fiery shade of persimmon. I open my mouth to ask if anyone needs any help.

"Don't forget the reason you dragged us in here." The man's quiet request makes my nape prickle, and I shut my mouth, conscious of my back molars grinding.

"I won't, babe, don't worry." Her tone strikes me as placating. Another hair-raiser.

"Someone needs to worry about how you spend your money." His voice is low and I have to strain to hear his words, but one surreptitious glance at his body language is all I need. He has both hands on his hips, glaring at Verity. His dog's tail is as still as the air on this humid day.

"You're the last one to talk about money." Verity's expression is twisted into a sneer, her tone harsh, but her arms are crossed over her middle. Protecting herself.

"We're talking about you, dear, remember?" He says "dear" like a verbal slap. "You're the one in the habit of wasting our hard-earned cash on stupid junk. Nothing is ever enough for you." While he keeps his volume low, it's not low enough. From his expression and total focus on Verity, he doesn't realize I can hear him. I'm catching his words and worse, their implied menace, loud and clear.

Do I have a supersensitive awareness of men who behave inappropriately? Heck, yes. Not from my deceased husband, Tom. He was all I'd ever dreamed a spouse could be and never treated me with anything less than total respect. We had our disagreements, though, same as any couple. They probably didn't look so great either, to an onlooker. My wariness comes more from my years in the Navy, though, where every now and then I encountered latent, and even blatant, misogyny. Not enough to sour my sense of pride and satisfaction at having served the country. Rather, enough to pick up on an asinine attitude before others might.

Which is why I'm working hard to not form a judgment against this man who I'm assuming is Verity's husband. It's hard for me to believe the other half of the town's most popular chiropractic practice would be so mean.

The Stonebridge Buddies is our local version of a Rotary Club. There are two chiropractors in the Buddies, Verity

Price and Hank Price. I've only ever seen Verity at the meetings, though. She's always bubbly and exudes a sense of quiet knowing. Nothing like the air of impatience Hank reeks of.

Be nice.

To his credit, he has a sweet dog who's behaving like an angel. A jerk wouldn't have a such an apparently loyal dog, would he?

Chapter Two

VERITY'S ARGUMENT WITH her husband is none of my business, but keeping my shop upbeat and a respite from the harsh grind of real life is. Time to break up their tête-à-tête before more customers enter.

I clear my throat. "Can I help you, Verity?"

Verity turns and faces me, her eyes bright. "Oh, yes, of course! Hank's just browsing, but I do have a question."

Hank shifts on his feet, and the dog stands up from his sit. No sense in allowing the rude dude to keep his sweet dog from affection.

"May I pet your dog? Can he have a treat?"

"Ah, sure." Verity's watching me as I take a treat from the canister we keep chock-full for our canine visitors. I have a separate sealed bin with tiny cat treats, too. "I'm not sure if you've ever met my husband, Hank?"

"Nice to meet you, Hank. I'm Angel." I nod at Hank, then hold up the treat, catching the Lab's attention. "And this is?"

"Moose," Verity answers, which I find a little weird as Hank stays quiet, aloof. A lot of husbands aren't overly thrilled with trinket shopping, and I understand. But few are so rude about it.

"Here you go, Moose." I drop the treat and Moose grabs it out of the air, forcing a bubble of laughter up my throat.

"Those are some fast reflexes, Moose!" I grin.

"Verity, we've got to get going." Hank's impatience is evident.

"Yes, I know." She shoots him a glare before she looks at me, her cheeks flushed. "I was wondering if my order is in yet?"

"We can check."

"It's the Japanese lantern I ordered right after Christmas, during your 50-percent-off sale."

"Yes, I remember." I walk over to the register and start searching for the shipment status.

Verity Price is one of my best customers, but she's also the most fastidious. No detail misses her bright-blue gaze, and she's quick to return something she changes her mind about. I have a generous return policy because I really do want my customers to be satisfied with their purchases. My desire is for each piece to become the customer's treasured keepsake, something that lifts their soul if only for a second.

This is one of the reasons I opened Shop 'Round the World. I want to share the international experiences I had while the Navy sent me all over the globe, family in tow.

"It's hard to believe it would take almost six months. Japan's not that far away, is it?" Verity's comment jerks me out of my reverie. I print out the most recent shipping status.

"It's a shame you still don't have your Santa gift, Ver." Hank speaks from across the store. He's casually inspecting a shelf of chess sets, with particular focus on a cartoon-themed board. When I make eye contact with him, he offers a self-effacing smile. "I'm Santa Claus. I bought Ver a gift card from you because she said this is her favorite shop."

I have zero recollection of him purchasing the gift card, but Christmastime was when I had the grand opening, and my daughters worked the store often throughout their university break.

The sleigh bells on the shop door chime and a customer wanders in, offering a quick smile before she starts perusing.

"I'm so sorry about this, Verity. Delivery times have been way off this year."

"Santa could have brought it faster on his sleigh." Hank's moved on to the Matryoshkas, wrestling open an eleven-piece literature-themed doll with what appears to be no concern for whether he damages it or not. He snorts when he gets to the last piece. It's a tiny cat with a wily grin, the perfect ending to something inspired by Bulgakov's *The Master and Margarita*.

He looks at me, puzzled. "What is this about?"

"It's a novel written during Stalin's terror in Russia. Bulgakov risked his life to do it."

"Huh." If I expected his interest to pique, then it's my problem that I feel disappointment as he scans the other dolls, still holding the tiny cat.

Losing interest, he puts the doll back, but not nested. "I'll be waiting outside, Ver. In the car. With Moose."

"Thanks, Hank. I won't be long." Verity looks over her shoulder at her husband, and I'm probably reading into it with a grumpy attitude, but is that a warning glance he's giving her? As in, she had better not take too long?

I keep the smile on my face but my fingers tap on my tablet more forcefully as my patience thins. The bells sound as he firmly shuts the shop door behind him and Moose.

I didn't imagine the man's overbearing presence. The shop's energy is lighter without him. Maybe I should ask Eloise, our local yoga shop owner and consultant for all things metaphysical, to get the negative vibes out for me.

Be nice.

"You're right, Verity. Your lantern should be here already. Give me one more sec, please, and I'll get this straightened out." I look around the shop; there's still only the one other customer, and she's sifting through the assortment of custom loose tea blends. I can escape to the back. The printer's in my office, down a short hallway and to the right. As I snatch the paper off the plastic holder, I notice the cup of iced coffee I made…two hours ago. What I wouldn't give for a cold brew from Latte Love up the street. And maybe a quick hi to Nate, my boyfriend and owner of the single independently owned coffee shop downtown. We're not serious in any kind of official way, but there's nothing casual about our relationship, either. We're both moving forward with our lives after enduring and healing from major losses. We're taking it slow. Not to mention we're each running our own local business, no small time sink.

I rush back to the front of the store.

"Here you go." I hand Verity the shipping statement and wait while she reads it. Her dress is impeccable: a two-piece pink-linen jacket and skirt set that reminds me of the women wearing Chanel in the streets of Paris, only cooler and more relaxed. I wonder if she came from a business meeting or if she gets this dressed up for Saturday errands. I place her somewhere around my age. Which means midforties, plus or minus ten. It's so hard to determine chronological age since the advent of modern dermatology, and I always feel as though I look older with the sun damage twenty years of Navy flying gifted me. Not that knowing ahead of time that my career path was going to add some wrinkles to my fair skin would have stopped me. I had my dream job longer than most people stay in one position. Piloting a helicopter on and off ships for a career will always be a highlight of my life.

"It says it's due to Middletown, on a delivery truck, by Monda," she reads aloud before lifting her gaze to mine again. While her tone is disappointed, her eyes reveal a different emotion. A vulnerability that I'm not used to seeing in her. She's probably embarrassed that I witnessed her altercation with Hank.

"Yes. So while we can't expect them to deliver today, I'm hopeful that early next week I'll be giving you a call that it's here. I'll have it delivered to your home within an hour of receiving it, promise. I am so sorry about this, Verity. I'll make it right."

"It's just that..." Verity's voice wavers.

"Yes?" I'm not immune to her emotions, but I'm not clicking with being on the verge of tears over a Japanese concrete lantern, even a custom-made one. My hunch that Hank's presence has something to do with her distress gains steam.

"It's for my birthday. Our birthday, actually. I wanted to surprise Hank with it. We're both turning forty next week."

"Oh, how fun. You share the same day?"

She nods. "And year. Although I know people think Hank married an older woman." A quick smile cuts through her apparent misery, but it's the fake kind that you do because you think everyone else finds something amusing that *hello*, no way do you.

"You make a beautiful couple." I mean it. If I hadn't witnessed their exchange, I'd have thought they were the picture of happy. "Look, you'll have the lantern for your birthdays. I'll drive to Middletown myself, if I have to, and get your lantern off the container truck." I silently pray I won't have to, as the lantern weighs 207 pounds, according to the invoice.

Verity sniffs, whips a pink tissue out of her coordinating

floral-print pale-pink leather tote, and dabs her eyes. "I'm sorry. I know this is definitely a very privileged problem to have."

"And I'm sorry that something you cared enough to think so far ahead about is causing you to stress." I rack my mind for the ideal compensation, since she's such a loyal customer. But I don't want it to look like I'm trying too hard, either. Logistics have been jammed up on a global level; there's nothing any retailer can personally do about it. Still…

I reach under the counter and pluck one of several Latte Love gift cards that I purchased for this very reason.

"I know it's nothing compared to having your lantern here already, but please get yourself a coffee, or tea, on me. I'm so sorry for your troubles, and I so appreciate your business."

Verity reaches up to accept the plastic card at the same moment a loud whistle sounds outside. Her hand shakes and she drops the card. My first instinct is that Ralph's whistling for me, signaling from his cage perch in front of the upstairs street window. But I know it's not his whistle. This one's more shrill, less musical.

Verity kneels down and grabs the card from the hardwood floor just as a second whistle pierces the shop's quiet. She straightens so quickly that she bonks her head on the edge of the counter.

"Oof!"

"Oh my." I rush around to her. "Are you okay?" Visions of blood spray cross my mind, and I force the nasty images away. Ever since I found Frannie's body in this same building last fall, I see murder around every corner. My evening pastime of bingeing true crime docudramas doesn't help. "Here, take my hand."

"Thank you but I'm fine, truly. I've got to go." She all but races to the door, swerving around two large display tables with an adeptness I'd never manage in such high wedge sandals. Verity turns back to catch my eye and holds up the gift card. "Thank you for the coffee!"

I wait for the door to shut behind her before I walk up to the large front shop window. Maybe I can see who on earth whistled for her like that. Her slim figure moves a bit jerkily as she jogs up to a black Mercedes SUV that's idling curbside. Verity crosses in front of the hood and gets into the passenger side. The car darts out into traffic before she closes her door, earning an indignant beep from the powder-blue Fiat it cut off. The Mercedes speeds up as it passes, but I'm able to see the driver without a problem. Hank Price, Verity's husband, is behind the wheel. I catch a glimpse of Moose in the back seat. I blink. The profile of the Labrador retriever signals that maybe Hank was whistling for Moose. Except, Moose was with him and already buckled in before Verity left the shop. I tell myself again, futilely, that Hank can't be that bad if he's a dog owner, right?

Wrong.

The jerk actually whistled for Verity like *she* was the dog.

My encounters with Verity—from when she came into Shop 'Round the World during the grand opening, until today—have been positive. She comes in weekly and rarely leaves without either purchasing or ordering a sizable item. So yes, my impression of her could be skewed a bit by the fact she's helping me make a profit. Even still, she was out of character today. Her consternation over the late delivery is fair. Watching her treat her husband with kid gloves, seeing the humiliation in her expression, hearing that dang whistle, is off the charts bizarre.

Maybe I'm wrong. Maybe Hank was whistling for the heck of it. But Verity's reaction told me all I need to know. She's under the thumb of a bully.

I stare at the car as it drives down Main Street, until it makes the left that would take them to their home in Cumberland Valley. Verity's address is well known in Stonebridge, as the formerly dilapidated Victorian estate has been infused with her tasteful eye and the couple's deep pockets. So impressive is their total redo of the house that it has been featured on all sorts of media outlets, including the fixer-upper channels and a few spreads in home and living magazines. I haven't personally seen any of this; I'm going off what my sister, Crystal, told me.

Verity and Hank Price are the doctors behind Price Chiropractic, two chiropractors who have a complete monopoly of all things spine-related this side of the Susquehanna River.

If you throw your back out in this town, you have two choices. Verity or Hank. Sure, you can drive the thirty minutes across the river and into Harrisburg, where you'll have your pick of practitioners. But when back pain's got me doubled over, I know I'm going to shop local.

My back's been complaining about the abuse it took while I was in the Navy, and my entire family raves about Verity and her talents with the human spine. No one has ever recommended Hank, now that I think about it. I've heard he's more the business half of their partnership. That makes sense to me after witnessing how he spoke to his spouse. I can't imagine a surly attitude would translate to a good bedside manner.

A quick rap on the window startles me. A warm rush of affection washes away my troubled thoughts when I recognize the owner of the strong knuckles.

Nate. And standing next to him, his ridiculously bushy tail wagging, is Mach—short for Macchiato—the Shiloh shepherd. Mach sports his Phillies baseball leash and collar set today, with a matching bandana embroidered with the fuzzy green team mascot, the Philly Phanatic. It would be overkill on any dog under 100 pounds. Since the wolflike canine is pushing 115, it works.

Nate's holding two clear plastic cups with Latte Love's logo stamped in royal blue, two matching blue-and-white-swirled paper straws inserted through the lids, the contents a creamy shade of mocha. *How lucky am I?* Three of my favorite things—Nate, cold brew, and Mach—are right on the sidewalk in front of me. I motion for Nate to come inside and greet them at the door.

"What a nice surprise! I didn't think I'd get to see you today." I gratefully accept the drink he holds out. "Hi there, Mach."

Mach wags his tail, which could be a dangerous thing considering its size and the fragile nature of much of my merchandise. But we're in the most open part of the shop, and all that Mach's bushy greeting does is whip up a welcome breeze.

"My new hire is covering for me, so I can't stay." Nate leans in and kisses me on the cheek. The imprint of the warmth from his lips makes me smile, and I know I'm beaming as though I'm obsessed with Nate. As though we're a lot more than close friends or casual dating partners.

The thing is, I think we are. That is, we might be. Getting closer, that is.

"Can you stay for a few minutes, at least?" I ask as we walk to the service counter. My single customer has moved past the glass bead display, her basket filled with an assortment of Czech cut crystal, and is carefully examining the damask table linens I just got in from Portugal. They were a last-minute buy a few months ago.

"For you, madame, I can stay for five minutes. To be fair, if you hadn't stolen away my store manager, I'd have longer to...hang out." Nate's smile makes my heartbeat trip in a way no cold brew ever has. I take a long sip of my drink, all the while studying the epitome of a silver fox standing in front of me.

"Amy was ready for a change. Besides, she's still handling all of your social media." Amy works for me as my website and social media guru, as well as at the register several hours each week. Her presence has freed up my time to focus more on what I'm best at, which is curating and ordering merchandise. Both Nate and I farm out whatever we can with our small businesses.

I savor a second sip of the cold brew. "I swear you read my mind. The iced coffee I made this morning died a sad, watery death in my office hours ago."

"Don't I always? You usually come in for coffee around ten, when you have someone else at the register. When you didn't show up, I figured you were busy. Plus"—he leans in, close enough that I catch a whiff of fresh roasted espresso— "I missed you."

"I'm glad you did. Stop in. I've missed you, too."

I've set up a pretty extensive beverage station in my back office, where I make all kinds of loose-leaf tea, drip coffee, espresso, and the infrequent hot cocoa. It's the perfect nook to talk business as needed, too. It's so nice when someone else makes me a tasty drink. Doubly so when it's Nate.

"Has it been a busy morning?"

"More interesting than busy. I'll fill you in later." I don't want to waste these precious few minutes talking about

Hank Price.

"Sounds good to me." He sips his coffee as I do mine.

"I have to say it, Nate. When it's hot out, nothing beats your cold brew."

"It's the nitrogen."

"It's more than that. Your roast is perfection." Latte Love specializes in nitro-infused cold brew, which takes the iced coffee experience into the stratosphere. "I'm so impressed with your vision, Nate. I need some of that with my store."

"You've got more than enough vision. I'd guess that winnowing down your inventory is the hard part. You have the world to choose from. I stay focused on one coffee growing area at a time."

"Hence your single origin, organic beans."

"You have been listening to my ramblings." He places his hand atop mine on the counter. "And I thought it was my pretty eyes." Nate's eyes glow with the same warmth that's dancing around my insides.

"To be fair, it's a little bit of both," I say.

Nate laughs, his smile emphasizing the lines around his eyes, his mouth. All signs of a man who isn't afraid to show some emotion. "Are you still going tubing with Bryce today?"

"Yes. As soon as Amy gets here."

"What about the girls?" He's referring to my nineteen-year-old twins, Ava and Lily.

"Lily's helping Crystal in the flower shop, and Ava already had plans with a friend from Pitt who lives in the area." It's wonderful having the girls home for their summer break, but they're each working two seasonal jobs, along with helping me out whenever they can fill in. Add in their blossoming social lives and it doesn't leave a lot of mother-daughter time. I'm okay with it for the most part, but I would like to get in a quick weekend away somewhere, just the three of us, before they return to school in August.

"Make sure you use bug spray. Mach and I got bombard-ed on the trail this morning. I took three ticks off him afterward." Mach's tail thumps on the hardwood floor. A Shiloh shepherd is an uncommon breed that's officially a mix of German shepherd and Alaskan malamute. I personally believe there's a good dose of wolf thrown in, but I have been accused of hyperbole. And did I mention the stand-up comedian traits? Because Mach's behavior can seem idiotic, bumbling, but then he'll stun with an example of brilliance that's too keen to be coincidence.

"We're not going to be on the trail, and the breeze on the water is almost always decent enough to keep the skeeters away." Both Nate and I are referring to the Appalachian Trail, accessible only two miles from Stonebridge. A smaller path branches off the AT and circles an area next to Jacob's Run, also popular for dog walking.

Our town is nestled in the foothills of the Cumberland Mountains and is an ideal location for any outdoor enthusi-ast. Of course, most of us are raised to believe this, out of practicality. When you're in the middle of what was until recently known as "cow valley," your parents have to use some imagination to keep your kiddie expectations for entertainment reasonable, not to mention affordable.

"Ticks with Lyme disease don't care about any of that. They'll drop out of the trees you're going to be floating under just as easily." Nate's expression is serious but I see the glint in his eyes.

"Please tell me you're yanking my chain."

"Caught." He winks, holds his hands up, palms forward. "Hey, you can't blame a guy for wanting to learn more about his love interest."

I blush when he uses the *l* word, but not out of any kind of bashfulness. We haven't gotten to anything more serious than "see you tomorrow" but it's there between us, this growing connection that's somewhere between warm affection and the kind of deep emotions that beg for a commitment. "And you can't blame me for thinking you're underestimating my safe tubing abilities."

His laughter is low and unaffected. "I admit it, I'm intimidated by your superpowers, every last one of them. Not all of us went to the Naval Academy."

We banter back and forth until the single customer approaches the register. Nate gives me a quick nod.

"Text me when you're back from your float. Think about what you'd like for dinner, too. Promise?"

"Promise." Another wink and he heads for the door. Saturdays are often our time to have a dinner together, prepared at either of our places. We both enjoy going to restaurants, but weeks are long for small business owners and a quiet night in is the ticket. An added bonus is that we live within a stone's throw of one another.

Still, there's a tug on my heart as the bells jingle when Nate closes it behind him. He's become a cherished part of my life.

The customer standing in front of me and the arrival of Amy for her shift distract me from further thought. I'm hoping time with my brother will shake off the vestiges of Hank Price's bad vibes.

Chapter Three

S LATHERED IN A megalevel SPF and ready for some serious chill time, I park next to my brother's vehicle in the lot adjacent the Jacob's Run and pop the car's trunk. Checking to make sure I have my sunglasses and hat, I walk between our cars to the tail end. I spot my brother and freeze. It's rare that I'm stunned speechless, but Bryce has done it.

"What?" Bryce's eyes, the same round shape and shade of hazel as mine, widen in hyperbolic shock. He's generously covered himself in opaque sunscreen, the white sheen not quite as blinding as the sun reflecting off his neon-yellow rash guard. My gaze lands on his rooster-print swim trunks and I look away, bite the inside of my cheek. "C'mon, Angel. What's so funny? You're laughing at me just like you used to when we were kids."

"I'm not laughing *at* you, Bryce. I'm laughing *with* you."

"I'm not laughing." He gives a perfect clown frown.

"You have to admit, you look like you're more ready for the shore than Jacob's Run." I nod at his unicorn inflatable, then hold up my sports tube, far more rugged and able to handle the sharp rocks that line the creek bed. "You said we were going tubing, right? In Jacob's Run? Unless you've decided we're headed to the township pool." I snortle, my version of a tiny giggle capped with a snort.

"Chillax, Sister." He tosses the smiling unicorn at me. "Catch. This is Uma, and she's our beverage attendant. I've got one just like yours for me." I grab the inflatable by its rainbow horn. Bryce's head disappears into the back of his red Fiat. He emerges with a large Styrofoam cooler and a wide grin. "Sparkling water, soda, electrolyte juice."

"We're going for two hours, not two days, Bro." I hold up my water bottle. "I didn't think past water, to be honest. I appreciate your thoughtfulness, though."

"You bet. You know you'll thank me when we leave the shade. Water's not quite as tasty."

"You're right about that."

We're at the far end of the parking spot that's used mostly by locals. Hidden from the street that runs alongside the edge of town, it's easy to think we're in the thick of the woods on the Appalachian Trail, when in fact we're mere steps from putting our tubes into the water and shoving off on our own little bon voyage.

"I hope you pretreated that." Bryce's bear paw of a hand motions at me, or more accurately, my pale skin.

"Yes, sir, with both sunscreen and bug spray. Nate urged me to use bug spray. Not for mosquitoes, either, but ticks. He said that he took ticks off Mach when they got back from the AT this morning. I thought that was unusual. It's not like they were walking through grassy fields."

"It's not unusual for Pennsylvania. We're the Lyme capital of world, sweetie. We just weren't as aware of it when we were younger." Bryce shuts his car and makes sure the lock chirps. We'll text Nico to pick us up three miles downriver, which may take as long as three hours or as quick as one. Usually it's more like two hours. Today may prove faster, though, as the creek looks a little high and the current's constant gurgle is audible.

"Please, no talk of how the years have flown. I want to enjoy the moment."

"Aww, are you feeling a little nostalgic? Or melancholy?"

"Neither, and I want to keep it that way. Ruminating on the past doesn't work for me."

I bend over to make sure my water sandals are fastened snug enough to stay on, but not so tight as to give me blisters. I'm wearing a tankini top with swim shorts. I know a T-shirt would have been smarter with the sun factored in, but summer's not all that long in central Pennsylvania and I enjoy the heat on my shoulders. My waterproof 100 SPF sunscreen should keep me from burning.

"Ready?" He's slung a lightweight nylon backpack over one shoulder, the cooler and his tube under the other arm.

"As I'll ever be. Let's go!"

Like the two kids we once were, we waste no time getting out onto the water. Bryce huffs and puffs until we get into the water. My brother hasn't had the Navy mandating his physical fitness like I have, and his husband, Nico, is on his case to join the gym to enhance his cardiovascular fitness. But he's still graceful as ever in the water and has Uma filled with the cooler and our personal effects in no time. Everything except the Styrofoam cooler is sealed in plastic bags and attached to the humble Unicorn, or, erm, "Uma," with nylon lines and carabiners.

I plod into the water after Bryce connects Uma to his tube with another line. I'm startled by the current as the water ripples around my knees. "This is way deeper than last time!" Two weeks ago, we'd taken a practice run, only venturing a half mile downstream, in our basic tubes. It had gone dreadfully slow and we both came back with scratches on our bottoms.

"At least our butts shouldn't scrape the bottom this time," Bryce says.

"Hear, hear." We both complained about sore tailbones after that excursion.

Bryce hands me a second nylon cord that's attached to Uma, and I clip it to my tube. Without preamble I put my back to my tube and plop backward into it. For the first few seconds, I feel as helpless as a beached whale. There's nothing graceful about getting into an inflated tire-shaped piece of plastic. The trick is to completely relax and forget any notions of going anywhere anytime soon. The current is in charge, which is the point. Nevertheless it's impossible to stop my grimace, or laughter, as all four of my limbs stick out and my bottom gets wet.

"We're off! Come on, Uma!" Bryce's cry makes me laugh again, and it's as if we're thirteen and eleven, sneaking out while Crystal is supposed to be babysitting us. We took advantage of her inattention more than once or twice, whenever she was on the phone with her high school boyfriend.

We make like ducks and use our hands to paddle away from the creek bank, into the deeper center where the current is strong enough to make tiny ripples around the rocks that peek their tops out of the deeper-than-usual water. South central Pennsylvania has had a deluge of rain over the last week, which has led to the mosquito infestation noted by Nate earlier. The brighter side of the frequent downpours is that we're moving along at a nice clip.

"This has to be the fastest it's been in years." Bryce lies back, arms splayed, face to the sun. "Look at the Trees of Heaven."

I squint at the bright sun that slants through the green lace canopy above us, the tree owning up to its name this afternoon. "You know that they're considered an invasive species, right?"

"Yeah, yeah, blah blah. Tree of Heaven also hosts the spotted lantern fly, blah blah." Bryce refers to the pest that's a bane for local agriculture. Just like the tree it lays its eggs on, the mothlike insect is beautiful and awe-inspiring to observe. The way they both crowd out and threaten other species? Not so much.

"Stop it." Bryce cuts through my thought fugue.

"What?" I feign innocence.

"Don't try to pretend with your older brother, Little Sis. You know better. Don't go down the spotted lantern fly, or invasive-anything road. Let it go, Sister. Let. It. Go."

I suck in a breath, ready to deny his astute observation that I'm BSing, but a giggle emerges instead. "For all you know, I've changed since I left home."

"Sure you have. We've all changed. But to be honest, honey? You've changed the most." Bryce shoots me a glance loaded with compassion. "It'd be impossible to not change after all you've been through."

My heart swells and I blink. The creek breeze must be irritating my eyes. Or maybe it's the pollen from the copious plant population. I sniff, swipe at my eyes. "Oh. Well, for the record, I wouldn't have been able to come back to Stonebridge and start my postnavy life without you and Crystal. Mom and Dad, too." My voice cracks.

"No weeping allowed unless you're a willow. I like how you shoved Mom and Dad in there at the end, by the way."

We both chuckle.

Our parents, Olivia and Douglas Strooper, are incredibly supportive and were loving parents. My siblings and I share a particularly strong bond, though forged amid Crystal's full adolescent breakdown complete with all the recreational drug use, Bryce coming out to the family in the mid-1980s when the concept of LGBTQ rights was still a dream, and me declaring I was going to leave it all behind to serve in the Navy. Crystal survived and found her better self in college, along with her better half, Brad. Bryce moved away to first New York, then London, where he met Nico. Nico had escaped a very traditional village in Southern Italy and they fell in love at first sight, at a London pub "near Knights Bridge Crossing on the tube's Piccadilly line." Bryce rarely misses an opportunity to recant their romance, in case you're wondering how I know so much about it. They relocated to Stonebridge not that long ago, and opened Skeins and Baahls to the delight of our mother, a lifelong knitter.

"I'm so happy you and I came back to Stonebridge, Angel. It's like the three of us are kids again, all back together, but without the teenaged angst."

"It was a lot more than angst, Bryce. You had no one to guide you. I at least had an older sister."

Bryce takes his time to answer. He's in the same relaxed prone position, his fingers dangling in the water. We're cruising at the pace that allows a cooling whisper of a breeze while preventing a total skeeter feast. I'm grateful I practically showered in DEET over my sunscreen, though.

"Oh, but I did."

"What?"

"I had a role model, a mentor. Mr. Adams."

"The high school librarian?"

"Yep. He never said anything more than 'You're okay just the way you are.' He told me to hang out in the library whenever it got tough. I ate many lunches with Brontë, Cervantes, and Dickens. It was a huge help to me those last two years of high school."

If it wouldn't risk stopping my smooth ride, I'd sit straight up. Someone had given my brother a hard time and I hadn't know about it? "Who was bothering you, in particular?"

"Stand down, Commander. It was never your fight, anyway, though I appreciate the sibling love. No one singularly bullied me, if that's what you're asking. That's the point. I was working so hard to fit in and not let anyone see that I was different. Mr. Adams saw me. I'm forever grateful. I looked him up about ten years after I graduated and told him in person. He was retired by then, but explained how he and his partner had to live a quiet life so as to not be harassed. He invited Nico and me to their wedding. They'd made a commitment years ago but renewed their vows when it became legal. Mr. Adams is a big reason I was amenable to moving back to Stonebridge. I hope I can mentor anyone who's struggling to find their way."

"I'm so glad, Bryce." Joy for my brother coats the bittersweet regret that I haven't been here for so much. My family's never treated me poorly for leaving, but living so far away for over two decades took its toll at times. We flew back every summer so that Mom and Dad would know Ava and Lily, now in college. And my parents visited us whether we were stationed in Washington, DC, only two hours away, or Misawa, Japan, a full day's travel to the other side of the world. But we never had the day-to-day, year-in year-out life of a family living in the same geographical area. Until now.

Bryce and I soak in the sibling serenity as we float along, allowing the water to carry us. There are other groups of creek floaters in front of and behind us, but they're all far enough away that it gives the impression that we have Mother Nature all to ourselves. I try to empty my mind of the shop's inventory, how to grow my customer base, worry over the twins and whether they're each happy with how their lives are going. I make a mental note to see when the girls and I can get together for a day, or at least an afternoon, for a girls' time. It's not easy finding a time that works between all of our responsibilities.

Boom.

The explosive sound comes from behind us, upriver. A bolt of anxiety shoots down my spine. I'm one of the lucky veterans in that my on-the-ground combat experience was minimal; I served more in the air save for a couple of missions that found me landing in a war zone. I don't suffer from the debilitating PTSD too many do. But hey, I'm a vet nonetheless and any explosive sound can set my teeth on edge. Especially when it intrudes on my serenity zone.

"What the heck?"

I look over at Bryce, who's watching me. Maybe a little

too closely. Does my family think I have PTSD?

"You're safe, Angel. We're okay."

"I don't have PTSD, Bryce."

"I didn't say you did."

"It's written on your face."

"Sorry, Sis. I'll never stop being your older bro." He shrugs. "That was a firework. Kids around here don't always wait for dark or the Fourth of July."

"It seems odd in the middle of a quiet afternoon is all. But I agree with you; that didn't sound like any gunshot I've ever heard." I lean back, and let the water's magic work. I may be atop an inexpensive float, moving down a local creek, but it's not much different from being in any one of the tropical paradises I've lived in. Hawaiian beaches, running into the warm surf with Tom and the girls, come to mind. Once the sun hits my skin and I can hear the gentle sound of lapping water, I'm in total Zen mode.

"Hey, look at that." Bryce points to signs staked on the Stonebridge side of the creek.

STONEBRIDGE HISTORICAL SOCIETY ARCHAEOLOG-ICAL AREA OF INTEREST

"Mom's been busy," I reply. Our mother is one of the town's most ardent supporters of establishing that there is an ancient eel weir in Jacob's Run. She's the de facto chairperson of the weir committee. A *weir* is an underwater structure composed of two stone walls that meet in a V, where Native

Americans captured eels. Eels were plentiful and a major source of nutrition millennia ago, and as recently as the past century when colonists and then European immigrants duplicated the Native American method. When the Jacob's Run weir was first discovered, many believed it to be a later model, a copy of the originals, since the ancient weir in the Susquehanna seemed to be the only one remaining in south central Pennsylvania. But upon further research and inspection, our mother discovered that there's a good chance "our" weir is indeed an archaeological treasure. The Pennsylvania version of an Egyptian pyramid.

"Olivia Strooper is a force of nature. How many retired schoolteachers would work longer hours after they left the classroom?" Bryce says. Crystal and I accuse him of being a mama's boy, and he is, but not in the revolting way. He simply loves his mother. We all do. Our parents are the salt of the earth, one of the main reasons I returned to Stonebridge. None of us are getting younger, and I don't want to miss time with them. Of course now they're constantly traveling and so involved with their various interests that I don't see them nearly as often as I'd imagined I would, but it beats only once a year.

"Mom's not afraid to put herself at risk from the naysayers, that's for sure," I agree.

Last November when my high school friend Frannie was found murdered in my shop, it was easy to see the anti-weir/antitourism proponents as suspects. Stonebridge has its share of vociferous citizens who don't want to see any more tourists flooding our town than already do. They want our town to be their own private paradise. Frannie, a top real estate agent, had been all about putting Stonebridge on the map as a prime Northeast tourist and resort destination. In the end, her death wasn't attributed to opposition to her big commercial dreams for Stonebridge, but the fact that it was even a possibility gave me concern for my mom. Still does.

"We might want to start planning a party for when she proves it's the real deal ancient wonder of central PA." Bryce is all about celebrations. Walking into Skeins and Baahls feels like stepping into a holiday-themed party, whether it's Christmas, the Fourth of July, or Veterans Day. He's arranged their yarn stock in rainbow color order, for instance, and riffs off that for whatever hue matches a particular season. While Christmas is my favorite season, Bryce and Nico's autumnal merchandising steals the show with its shades ranging from bright orange to golden amber.

"Do you think they're any closer to figuring out the actual age of the weir? I missed the last Buddies meeting. Did they mention when the PSU archaeological department is supposed to start diving on the weir?" I ask.

"Soon. The paper said by August, but at the Buddies meeting they announced by the end of this month, so who really knows?" Bryce lets his hand skim the water as we float, the creek moving a little faster than the painted turtles that cross the roads around here this time of year.

"I wonder how long it'll take to determine its real age."

"No telling. But I'm betting it's indeed ancient. I have a hard time believing that Jacob Stoner built it." Bryce sounds so authoritative I can't help but laugh.

"You were a corporate dude and now you're a fiber artist. What on earth would you know about a man who lived over two centuries ago?"

"Hey, I do more than knit. I read. And there's a great YouTube video about the Susquehanna weir." He adjusts his wide-brimmed hat so that it covers his face as he leans back against his tube. "Jacob Stoner was a heck of a leather tanner, and his wife made a mean pigeon pie. But the cabin he built for them still stands only because it's been reinforced over the years, thanks to the historical society's fundraising. Jacob Stoner was a man of many talents, but construction? Not so much. Something underwater would have required, I don't know, a stonemason to build it."

"I'm sure there were such experts in that first wave of settlers. He and his wife weren't alone for long."

"Hmph. Doubtful." Bryce's voice drifts and I close my eyes. The sun's heat intensifies as we clear the shade of the overhanging trees.

A sudden, sharp tug on the left side of my tube sends me into a slow spin. I sit up, wondering why I'm suddenly moving backward, toward the bank. Bryce curses and starts splashing.

"What's going on?" My heart's pumping irrationally

hard. My internal scanner, my situational radar, has been on overdrive since Frannie's murder.

"I can't move!" Bryce screams. My heartbeat thuds in my throat, as I'm already on alert from the firecracker. Have I been a fool to think the creek is a safe place?

Chapter Four

"CALM DOWN A minute. What's going on?" I put my Navy training to work. One of us needs to stay focused and it's not going to be my brother, who looks like a caricature of his cartoonish self.

"Uma's hit a snag. I can't get her to move, not without risking a tear."

"God forbid Uma sinks," I deadpan.

He grunts. "Let me get up and fix it." He twirls his beefy arms around, his belly baring itself between his KNITTING KEEPS ME FROM STABBING PEOPLE T-shirt and his print Bermuda swim trunks. "I'm stuck! Damn tube."

"Hang on!" I flip myself out of my tube. I land on all fours, the water lapping my shoulders. Sharp gravel stabs into my knees, my palms. Scrambling to my feet, I discover the water's close to thigh-deep, and not as easy to walk through as it was closer to shore because the current is stronger. All three floats are connected by the nylon line and carabiners. I inspect the lines one by one, from my tube to Bryce's, from Bryce's to Uma. Now that I'm out of my float, it's bobbing atop the water, going nowhere fast. Bryce's line to Uma is taut, keeping us from going anywhere as long as the unicorn inflatable is stuck.

"Hang on. I'll get Uma. Don't let go of the line, and don't tug on it. She's right in the middle of the dig area. Probably stuck on a rock," I say. Our inflatable cooler holder is in a precarious spot. She's tilted at an angle, and I'm not certain the cooler's intact but I keep my observation on the down-low. I don't want to get Bryce more worked up than he already is.

"I won't let go, trust me. First, help me up!"

"Fine. Heaven forbid I do it all myself." I sigh, very dramatically if you ask me, and wade to my brother. One annoying thing about returning home is that no one seems to realize that I do have a fair amount of life skills that don't require a sibling's or parent's help.

"Here." I hold out my arms.

He reaches up for my hands, and I employ all I know about bending my knees and using my legs, not my back, to tug him to his feet.

I lean back as far as I can, and Bryce begins to lever out of his tube. For a precarious second, we're suspended over the creek, Bryce half out of the tube and me hovering over the water's surface. It's as though we're doing an ice-skating trick on our frozen backyard pond, except we're forty-five and forty-seven, not eight and ten. But leverage wins and Bryce stands up straight, relieved of his temporary immobility. I let go of his hands and shake out my arms.

"Oh, my back!" Bryce cries out the minute he's upward and clutches his lower spine.

"Stand still, take a deep breath." I know from hours in a helicopter seat that lower back pain is no joke. "Where does it hurt?" I step closer, ready to massage whatever's cramping.

"No, please, don't touch." He's speaking in a whisper. "It's my sciatica." He whispers the word as though he's saying "bubonic plague." He turns his head toward me, and his grimace says it all. Uma or no Uma, our float trip is over before it began, dang it.

"It's okay, we'll get you home. You'll be fine. Can you stand up straight?"

He grasps my hand again and I use my core (thank you, yoga class) to center myself, slightly bending my knees so that I don't mess up my spine, too. Slowly, slowly, Bryce stands up, sweat pouring down his face. He's really done it this time.

"Okay, now, stay here and I'll pull Uma free. Then we'll walk over to the creek bank together, okay?"

"Yes." His eyes are closed, his face pale, but his voice is strong, hands on his hips. He's thrown his back out before and I know he'll cope.

I scan the area, and note that we're alone out here, and halfway between the two shores. Uma is stuck about fifteen yards closer to the north side. "Tell you what, if you can start walking, follow me when you're ready. I'll get Uma and we'll get out over there." I point to a shady area under a large willow tree with low-lying branches.

"Okay. Just go. I'll get there."

"Are you sure you're all right for now?" I don't want him to hurt more than he has to.

"Yes. Please. Go," he whispers.

Don't have to tell me twice. I slosh on over toward Uma, my tube dragging behind me. I've clipped my end of the line to the back of my fanny pack, where my phone's stashed in a plastic bag. This kind of situation is exactly why I'm so careful about taking my phone and keeping it dry. I look over my shoulder to make sure my motion isn't pulling on Bryce's tube yet. True to his word, he's holding his end of the line firmly, and has it attached to his shorts, too. There's a lot of slack, so I keep walking.

I'm where the right side of the weir begins and notice more signage that we didn't see while floating. The signs face the shore and warn that the area is off-limits to anyone but the Penn State archaeological department. "Mom really has been busy—there are Penn State signs here, too. Did you know that?"

Bryce doesn't reply, and from the way his face is pinched in pain, he may not have even heard my observation. Poor guy.

As I approach Uma, I see that she's tilting because her right side is deflated. Her head is folding backward, making her unicorn horn look like...well, let's say her horn looks odd.

"What on earth did you get stuck on, girl?" I know, talking to inanimate objects seems weird but it's a holdover from my Navy pilot days, when my helicopter was indeed my best friend. At least during a mission.

Uma doesn't answer, of course, but I see that the front part of the tube is up against the sharp edge of a large rock, the same kind of miniboulder that sprinkles either side of the creek, making some areas off-limits to tubers and kayakers because of the hazard. Something white is sticking out from under Uma's belly, and I assume it's another fold of the deflating float.

I bend over, take Uma by her flaccid horn, and tug. No dice. She doesn't want any part of being set free, so I grab her neck, my slippery fingers digging into the deflating plastic. I hear a dismaying *rip* as I haul Uma out of the water, followed by a definitive *plop* that splashes water over both me and the float.

It's then that I see that the "something white" I saw a few seconds earlier, what has made the splash, isn't connected to the float. It's a hand.

A *human* hand.

I'm too shocked to scream but not so much that I don't immediately kick into rescue mode. Anticipating I'll be rendering CPR, I take stock. It's as though time stops as my gaze travels from said hand, up its arm, to the short sleeve of a T-shirt that's imprinted with PRICE CHIROPRACTIC HAS YOUR BACK. I gasp.

Hank Price lies prone, his eyes unseeing, floating atop Jacob's Run. On automatic, I press my fingers to his jugular, hold my hand over his nose and mouth. No air in and out, no pulse. His skin isn't any colder than the water, but it has a gray tinge to it. I look at his hand again, at his fingernails. They're a darker blue than I've ever seen, except…when Tom passed. My husband's nails turned dark blue, almost black, right away. A shocking reminder of death's finality. Which is why I know Hank is past the point of help.

There's nothing my emergency training can do for him now.

Hank Price is dead, a victim of… My mind starts churning. Have I mentioned I have a compulsion to know what killed someone? It was triggered by Frannie's murder last year. Or my binge-watching of cold case murder documentaries. Or maybe I was born this way.

I'm vaguely aware of sloshing but don't react until I hear Bryce's harsh gasp. "Is that—"

"Hank Price."

"And he's—"

"Dead, yes." I'm unable to stop staring at Hank's body. It's floating as if he stopped in the creek to cool off. He's even wearing sports sandals. And wrapped around his left wrist is a dog leash. I recognize the cording because Nate has the same style of leash for Mach.

My mind switches from what—Hank's dead body—to why. Is it possible that Hank was walking his dog, Moose, the very dog who was in my shop earlier?

When Hank was still alive? A detached part of my mind recognizes the emotional shock and shuts it down. Compartmentalization keeps warriors going through fire and it'll help me figure out what the heck is going on here.

Could Moose have hauled Hank off the path that runs alongside the creek, making him trip? Did Hank fatally hit his head?

I bend over to look more closely at his skull but remember I shouldn't touch or move a single thing. That's when I see the unnatural angle his head is tilted at. My stomach heaves.

"Don't touch him, for heaven's sake!" Bryce insists.

I straighten, take in huge gulps of air. "Don't you think I know that?"

"You looked like you were going to try to give him mouth-to-mouth. He's gone, honey. Dead." Bryce runs at the mouth when he's upset, and I understand. But my jaw doesn't as my teeth clench, and I have to stop myself from telling him to shut up. The chatter in my mind would put the most loquacious chipmunks to shame.

"Yes, he's gone." My stomach is still clenched. Just like it was after I found Frannie. I guess finding a dead body is like childbirth. The immediate visceral reaction seems forgotten, but it's been lurking there all along.

This isn't the same thing. Hank wasn't murdered, he had an accident.

I look at Hank again. And to the shore, no more than five yards away. A stretch of crushed brush runs from the bank and hiking path, several feet above the creek, to the water. Hank probably tripped, tumbled down, hit his head, and...expired. Yes, it was definitely some kind of unfortunate fall. Lethal. But not another murder. The chances of me finding a second murder victim in a lifetime has to be nil, right?

I have to call the police. Which for me means Trinity Colson, Stonebridge PD's lead detective.

"I need my phone."

"Don't you have it with you?"

"Yes." I fumble with my fanny pack, free the phone from the plastic bag.

"I'll bring in your tube while you're on the phone." Bryce grimaces as he steps toward the line connecting our floats.

"No, don't!" My Navy commander voice is in full force. "Like you said, the less touching, the better."

"Your float isn't attached to Hank."

"Uma's attached, er, *was* attached, to him. Which means we were, too. Stay here and watch the scene. Do not let anyone else come into the water. And if you see a large brown Lab, his name is Moose." Poor Moose. He can't have met the same fate—

Do. Not. Go. There.

"Got it." Bryce turns back toward the creek's edge, where

bushes and trees provide a decent screen from the hiking path. I hope it'll keep anyone from seeing what we already have. At least until the police get here. I notice Bryce put himself between Hank's body and the shore, and I've no doubt he comprehends the sacred duty we're tasked with. We need to give Hank respect and protection until the police get here. The enormity of what's happened hits me again and I stop, bent over my tube, breathe in through my nose, out through my mouth. I have to stay focused.

The police. Without further thought, I press the number for my friend. Trinity is one of my speed dials.

"Hey, Angel. What's up?" Trinity's light tone reveals she's in weekend mode, expecting me to ask if she wants to meet for a quick coffee or whatever. I'm about to break through her assumption.

"I—I—I…" I gag, the reality hitting me.

"Breathe, Angel. Are you safe?" Trinity makes the transition to law enforcement professional in a blink.

"Sorry, it's just that…I'm fine, it's not me." I start wading toward shore. The movement grounds me. "Hank Price isn't, though. He's dead."

Chapter Five

"I FOUND HIM floating in Jacob's Run, smack in the middle of the weir area—you know, where it's cordoned off? Near the north bank about a quarter mile from the Stone Cliff Park entry. We're at least a mile from the Conodoguinet." I use the larger Susquehanna River feeder creek as a reference point as I step ashore and relish the solid ground under my wet feet. My water shoes *squish squish* until I stop under a large willow tree and lean against it, ticks be damned. Its strong trunk supports my shoulders, my upper back. The semisquat position allows me to take in deep breaths.

"Yes, I know where it is. And I have your phone's location," Trinity says. "I'll be right there, and I'll send units. Anyone else with you?"

"Bryce." And a very deflated Uma tube.

I disconnect and lock eyes with my brother, who's also walked ashore but remains at the edge of the bank, his watchful gaze on the walking path. We've been lucky that it's turned into such a scorcher of a day. The heat keeps pedestrians away.

"Was that Trinity?" he asks.

"Yes. Help's on the way."

"Nothing's going to help Hank, poor fellow." Bryce's baleful expression echoes my sentiments.

"No."

"I hate to say it, Angel, but Trinity's not going to be happy about this." Despite his sciatica flare, he's still able to shake his head at me, as if all of this is my fault.

"Of course she's not. What person in their right mind is happy about a death?"

"I'm not talking about Hank. It's you. I mean, it was only, what, a few months ago that you found Frannie in your shop?"

"Seven. It was seven months ago." As if a month distanced me from whatever cloud's hanging over me.

I have to admit, finding my second dead body since returning to Stonebridge makes me wonder, too. Is there a reason corpses are drawn to me?

Am I exuding some kind of death vibe?

ONCE TRINITY AND the forensic team arrive, it's all business. The officers fan out over the scene, attend to Hank, and cordon off the area. Trinity doesn't waste time with small talk and asks me to tell her the story again.

"We were tubing, and Uma, I mean, Bryce's float, got

stuck. I came over to check it out, and Hank was floating there." I cast a quick glance over my shoulder to where five different people, three in uniform, are working, collecting evidence. One is busy with a phone camera, and another is using an actual camera set on a tripod. A man in bib waders bends down, removing him from view behind the large tarp-type screen SPD set up almost as soon as they arrived. I know it's the coroner, and he's examining Hank's body.

I shudder, wishing I was anywhere but here. If only this was all new to me.

"I know it's not as important as a dead body, but I'm worried about Moose. The dog. Since Hank's still holding his leash…"

Detective Trinity Colson, Stonebridge PD, because she's here in an official capacity, eyes me. Because we've renewed and can I say, made better, our best friendship from youth, I see the bemusement in her gaze.

"Moose is back home. That's all I can say." Trinity looks annoyed that she told me that much, but I'm relieved to know Moose is safe. He can offer comfort to Verity in this terrible time.

"Wait, so Verity knows—"

"She called in when the dog came home alone, off leash. She was concerned that Hank hadn't returned after two hours. No, she has not been informed of his death yet. Let's keep to your story for now, Angel."

"Okay." I tell her everything I can think to, including the

firework *boom*.

"What time did you hear the firework?"

"Maybe an hour, hour and a half before we found Hank?" I guesstimate. "I was startled by it and asked Bryce what he thought it was. It didn't sound like a gunshot, if that's what you're thinking." Could Hank have been murdered? *No.* Not here, in broad daylight, surely?

"What I'm thinking isn't important right now, Angel." Her lips are in a thin line.

"You're wondering if you can trust me, aren't you? You're worried I'll go off on my own and investigate."

"Not at all. And for the record, I trust you." She doesn't miss a beat. "I do wonder, though, how much trauma one person can handle. Navy helicopter pilot career aside."

"You're one to talk."

She looks away. We've already discussed, compared, analyzed our respective professions—hers as a homicide detective trained on the streets of Harrisburg, and my flight hours earned in combat zones—over our many girls' nights in, coffee talks, hiking the Appalachian Trail on our rare same days off.

"Let's get back to the task at hand." She motions to one of the uniformed officers.

"Ma'am?" The young woman's name tag states RODRI-GUEZ.

"Take notes for me." Officer Rodriguez starts tapping on a tablet. Trinity still uses pen and paper, and has her small notebook open.

"Again, Angel, tell me when you realized it was Hank Price?"

"Right after I saw the T-shirt. I've seen Verity wearing the same one numerous times. She gives them away at our Buddies meetings." I'm sad I haven't worn the aqua-blue shirt Verity gave me. We all do our best to support each other's businesses. "When will Verity be notified?"

"That's my next stop. Please don't call her, okay?" Trinity's writing with her pen.

"I wouldn't. I'm not even close to her. Trinity, you know me."

She grunts. I think if we weren't at a crime scene with a dead body she'd laugh, but Trinity has never shown anything but respect for everyone she meets, dead or alive. When she investigated the murder of our high school friend Frannie, Trinity treated Frannie's corpse as if she were still alive and hearing all we spoke about. And she didn't let go of a single thread of the investigation until we—actually, I figured out the killer first, but I couldn't have done it without Trinity's insight—solved the case and caught the murderer.

"Trin?" I don't want her to think I'm looking for special treatment but she has that stone face expression that sends shivers deep into my soul. "You know I just happened upon Hank's body, right?"

She purses her lips and rests her hands on her slim hips, the movement revealing the weapon under her pale-cream linen blazer. Although Trinity calls it a pistol, my Navy training doesn't allow me to think about a firearm as anything but a weapon or my sidearm. I've teased her about it before... *Why are my thoughts so erratic?*

Shock. It's the shock. No amount of training or experience can shake the trauma of seeing a dead body, especially one I saw alive mere hours earlier.

"It's hard to say what's going on. Most likely this is a freak accident, and a pure coincidence that you found another body. But on the other hand, if you were tubing on the same day, in most likely the same hour, as Hank Price was killed, that's different."

"But it was an accident, right?" I ask.

"That hasn't been determined yet."

"I admit that it does look odd, me being here and all. When I usually am in the shop. Except I don't know Hank Price. I only formally met him this morning. Bryce and I planned today's outing two weeks ago. I don't ever remember seeing Hank walking his dog this afternoon."

Trinity nods, asking what I assume are the usual questions given to witnesses, and Officer Rodriguez taps away on her glass screen. Trinity's questions are almost identical to the queries she asked when Frannie died. And back then she asked me to go to the station to give my report. At least this time it looks like I won't have to take the gratis ride in a cruiser's back seat.

"Okay, that's it for now. Thank you, Lucia," Trinity says

to Officer Rodriguez.

"Yes, ma'am." Officer Rodriquez looks at me. "Ma'am." I nod. She walks away.

"She seems nice."

"Nice and overworked, like my entire team." Trinity scans the scene, letting her shoulders down a bit. "We've been asked to support the surrounding towns in our county."

"Why? Is it the summer, all the tourists?"

She shakes her head. "Who knows what it is?" Which means Trinity's not at liberty to discuss it.

"I know I'm not the professional here, but I saw the dog leash Hank was, still is, holding. It looks like he was walking his dog. He has a Labrador retriever. I met him earlier today, when I met Hank. The dog's name is Moose. But Moose is a heck of a lot nicer than his daddy."

"Explain."

I summarize the scene inside and outside my shop. Trinity appreciates brevity, and I'm a master of keeping it brief. "Did you catch the part where he whistled at Verity like she was a dog? She'd used up her shopping time, apparently."

"There's a lot of assumptions there, Angel. You didn't witness Hank whistling, did you?"

"Well, no, but come on. Verity jumped to the ceiling when she heard it. And the way he sped away…" I can't help but glance toward his body, but it is behind a large plastic tarp that is staked to the creek bed, preventing the public from catching a glimpse. The coroner appears from behind the plastic and walks toward us, his somber gaze on Trinity.

"What have you got, Buck?"

Buck hesitates, his gaze bouncing between me and Trinity. Trinity gives him a curt nod. "It's okay. You can say whatever you need to say."

He nods. "Okay. Well, we won't have everything we need to know until after an autopsy, but it doesn't look like an accident. Not at all. Not with the hole in his chest, and exit wound in his back. And this." He holds up an evidence bag with a small object inside. It's the unmistakable shape of a bullet. "Officer Jones found it on the creek bank."

My stomach plummets. "What? It can't be murder. There wasn't any blood in the water. His head was twisted like a lemon slice on a glass of iced tea!"

Trinity glares at me the same moment I realize I spoke aloud. *Dang.*

"His head is at an odd angle against the rock is all I meant. Sorry." I hold my hand out to the coroner. "I'm Angel Warren. You probably don't remember me, but—"

He accepts my hand. Firm clasp, one shake. "Oh, I remember you, Angel. And Frannie, may God rest her soul." He frowns. "That was a shocker."

"It was. I'm sorry I said what I just did. About the lemon." Both Buck and Trinity have their granite expressions back in place, but I can't help myself as I press on. "It's just that it looked to me like Hank was walking his dog, his dog bolted, Hank was yanked off his feet. Isn't it possible he slipped, hit his head on the rock?" Every summer there is a tragedy on the Susquehanna River, located only a few miles downstream via Jacob's Run and Conodoguinet Creek. Usually the victim is an adolescent under the influence of booze or drugs. Sometimes it's an adult, like Hank. Alcohol and water sports don't mix well. "Maybe he had a cocktail at lunch and wasn't as steady on his feet as normal."

Buck shakes his head. "Normally I'd say you're probably right. But there's the bullet and the wounds." He turns away from me, but I don't miss the knowing glance he shoots Trinity. They need to talk alone. I get it.

"I'm leaving."

"Stay nearby. I'm not done with you," Trinity says.

I walk over to Bryce, who's giving his statement to Officer Sam McCloud. I met Sam when, you guessed it, the other murder happened. They both look up as I near, and Sam's eyes narrow. Yeah, he remembers me, too.

"Hello, Officer McCloud." I'm not going for casual first name right out of the chute.

"Ms. Angel Warren." He gives me a cursory smile before he turns back to Bryce. "If we need more, we'll ask you to come down to the station."

"Whatever you need, Officer."

With a curt nod to each of us, Sam walks toward Trinity and Buck.

"So much for our tropical float down Jacob's Run." Bryce lets out a sigh. His hands are on his hips and the lines on his face convey his discomfort. The detritus of our aborted mission—our stacked tubes, a flat Uma, the cooler we never cracked open—lies in a pile at his feet.

"Here, let me get you a drink." I squat down and raise the cooler lid.

"Thanks, Sis. Bending down isn't in my repertoire at the moment."

"Here." I pull out two sparkling waters, still cold, and hand him the blackberry-flavored one. I take the watermelon infused. We're quiet as we gulp the refreshments. I finish my bottle and reach for another. "Want another one?"

"Absolutely."

After we finish our second bottles, our gazes meet. My brother has that look that I'm all too familiar with. The one he had when I ran into his room for solace after catching my parents in the act. You know what I mean. They explained away what I walked in on with "we were doing our workout routine. Like gymnastics." I was six. I believed them, they were my parents, after all, but I'd still been traumatized to realize adults did *naked* gymnastics. Of course now I realize they were—*ick*. Can't go there, nope, never.

"Spit it out, Bro."

"Are you thinking what I'm thinking?" His brow rises.

"That we're dehydrated?" I hand him a third bottle of water.

"Please." He takes another gulp. "You know what I mean." He motions toward the ambulance where Hank, or rather, Hank's body, is being loaded. The starkness of the black body bag against the lush green shrubs and low-hanging trees makes my stomach plummet again.

"Am I wondering how he died? Not any longer. I heard what the coroner said. What he thinks."

"And?" Bryce asks.

"He thinks it's murder."

Chapter Six

SUNDAY MORNING I wake earlier than normal after a night of tossing. I found myself trying to piece together the who, whats, and whys of Hank's murder with zero satisfaction. I know the where, of course. And I know that the first person to look at is Verity, since she's his spouse. It's difficult to imagine the chiropractor holding a weapon of any kind, much less using it to kill her husband. She's a healer, not a killer. And as she is a customer who frequents my shop for the most elegant home and garden decor, I don't want to believe she'd do it.

I can't stop replaying Verity and Hank's interaction in the store, though. If I was married to a man who talked to me like that, well... I wouldn't murder him. It's too soon to even begin to figure it out, but unless there's a motive yet to be found, I'm leaving Verity on the maybe list only because I have to. I glance at the clock on the wall. It's not too early to call Trinity but it's also none of my business. Nor is this my crime to solve. Except...it is, as far as my overactive mind is concerned.

As I measure out the beans for the pot of coffee—I'll

have a cup and the girls will have the rest when they wake up—my mind goes back to Verity. She's all alone in that huge home on the edge of town. I know a lot about waking up without my husband beside me. Tom died of natural causes at an unnatural age. Way too young, yet I wouldn't want him to be alive a second more than he was, knowing the suffering his illness would have brought if he'd lingered.

I had time to mourn, to experience the empty rooms without him, to sleep in our bed, alone. But I wasn't totally alone because I had the girls. They were tweens and we were stationed in Hawaii. That's where we adopted Ralph, from the local avian rescue group.

Less than a year after Tom passed, I was offered orders to Belgium and I jumped on them. It was an opportunity for the girls and me to make some new memories, visit some of the places we'd been while Tom was still here, to move forward. Will Verity opt to stay in their home?

The grinder *whirs* the beans, and Ralph decides to join in the ruckus. He mimics everything from the microwave *beep* to a squeaky door hinge. His skill is so acute that he was a big part of helping me solve Frannie's murder last year.

"Ralph!" Ava's grouch shout stops Ralph midwhir sound, at the same time the machine transitions to brew mode. I leave the kitchen, which is part of the great room the renovations made the second floor into before and right after we moved into the old building. In addition to the large living room, kitchen, and dining area, the second floor has my master bedroom suite. Ava's sitting on the bottom of the stairs that lead up to the third level, where two bedrooms and my meditation/workout/yoga room are.

"Good morning, honey. I'm sorry that I woke you up."

"You didn't wake me, that green monster did." Ava loves Ralph as much as Lily and I do, but they do have the most friction between them. Ralph likes to try to nip her every now and then, despite the reality that Ava gives him the most treats.

"Awww, pretty bird." Ralph peers out from under his cage cover, wanting to be with us no matter the time.

"Okay, grumpy chicken." Ava climbs the rest of the way downstairs, her long legs bare beneath an oversized PITT UNIVERSITY T-shirt. "Why are you up so early, Mom?"

"Couldn't sleep."

"That's no surprise. You found a dead dude yesterday."

"Hank Price. He has a name, honey, and it turns out he was a murder victim."

"I'm sorry." Ava has the sharpest tongue of the twins, but she's the quickest to admit when she's overstepped. "Has Auntie Trinity found out anything?"

I can't keep the smile off my face. Trinity told the girls to call her "auntie" ever since she and I have rekindled our friendship. It's another reminder that I'm exactly where I belong. I'm home.

"Not that I know of, but I'm sure she's not slept a whole lot, either. The sooner we catch the killer—" I cut myself off, a little scared at how easily I said "we."

"Yeah. I thought living in Pittsburgh, or Philly like Lily does, would mean more crime. And statistically that's true, but it feels like Stonebridge has turned into a murder center," Ava says.

"Strike those words, please. Let's get some coffee."

"It smells good."

"It's Nate's newest, roasted this past week." I pour the hot liquid into our mugs and Ava takes a long sniff.

"Mmm. Caramel, maybe orange? It's definitely fruity."

"You could be a roaster. The bag says warm notes of burnt butter with citrus."

"Why doesn't it just say 'caramel'?"

"That wouldn't be so fancy, would it?"

We each pour half-and-half into the dark liquid, stirring with the spoons I picked up in the Czech Republic. They're petite with sterling silver–twisted handles and varied polished rocks at the ends of the handles.

Ava holds up her spoon, the one with the agate stone. "I didn't see these in the shop."

"No, I can't find them anywhere. Do you remember where your dad and I bought them?"

Her brow knits. "Prague, was it? Where we saw the C-section Barbie doll?"

"We were in one of the most beautiful cities of the world, with a medieval clock that still works in its town square, and you remember a toy museum." I chuckle.

Ava shrugs. "We were kids, Mom."

"You were." Twins are so interesting. Ava and Lily are identical, with a few physical disparities, but very different personalities. Ava's hair tends to fall more in the light-brown category and Lily's is dark blonde. They each have Tom's eyes, and my family's strong build. Their slapstick sense of humor is similar to the point of being annoying, especially when they get into one of their giggling spasms.

"Hey, guys." Lily shuffles into the kitchen and makes a beeline for the coffeepot. She's in an owl-print tank top. The owl is Temple University's mascot. This is what I mean about my twins. They're on the same frequency but different volumes.

"Good morning, honey bunny."

"Hellooooo." Ralph strains to make sure Lily sees him on Ava's shoulder.

"You're not making me jealous, Ralph." Lily helps herself to coffee and joins us. "Why are we all up at this hour on a Sunday? Let me guess. Mom couldn't sleep."

"Bingo," Ava says.

"I think you're a natural crime solver, Mom. I mean, with your Navy time. You can't expect to be happy with just running the shop all the time." Lily's nineteen but her steadfast gaze reveals an old soul.

"If I wanted to be a detective, or any kind of cop, I'd have done it. Crime doesn't interest me."

"Maybe not but murder does. Just take a look at your

Hulu and Netflix queues." Ava looks at Lily. "We were trying to find something funny to watch the other night, but because we were on your profile, it kept suggesting the sickest stuff."

Lily gulps half her mug in one go, sans cream. "I'm sorry, Mom. You've had your share of rough times since we moved here."

"Actually, I'm not the one having a rough time. It's the victims." But maybe they have a point. I am a bit compulsive about finding a killer. It's a primal impulse to me.

"You've always been a good puzzle solver, Mom. I dunno, maybe solving murders will be your eel weir," Lily says.

No way do I like being compared to my mother, and me solving murders to her weir escapades. I'm nowhere near retirement for good, nor will I ever look at solving a mystery as a hobby. But the girls have a point.

One I'm unwilling to examine. I clear my throat.

"Well, girls, speaking for myself, I'm enjoying it here more than I imagined. I know it's probably different for you both, since you were barely here last summer before you went off to college."

"It feels like home, though," Ava says. "As though we've lived here a lot longer."

"Anywhere Ralph is, is our home." Lily smiles. "I like that we're away at college but close enough to come home for all the breaks if we want."

"I was afraid you'd get bored over the summer, without

having friends you grew up with."

"Are you kidding? All of my new friends want to drive here and check out Stonebridge. Jacob's Run is a draw, with Grandma's ancient quest." Lily's enthusiasm reminds me that my daughters can take care of themselves.

"It's not proven ancient, not yet. Ava, did you say you have friends coming in town today?" I ask.

Ava nods, looks at her phone. "Yeah, I have to get into the shower." She stands and stretches. Ralph clings to her shirt.

"Because if your friends get one whiff of your pits, they won't be your friends for long," Lily pipes in.

"Shut up and shave your legs, Sister. Or should I call you Sasquatch?"

"You're one to talk!"

I sip my coffee and soak in our family's love, as smelly and hairy as it is.

LATE SUNDAY AFTERNOON, the sun slants through the redbud tree that grows at the corner of my sister's expansive back deck. I'm trying my darnedest to let go of yesterday's horror and enjoy what's meant to be a casual family barbecue. So far I'm unsuccessful at both.

"You have to admit, it's odd that Stonebridge has never had a murder, ever, until last November, when you found

Frannie." Brad, my brother-in-law, speaks from the grill. We're on their back deck, enjoying a rare summer breeze.

"And then you found Hank yesterday." Nico, my other brother-in-law, chimes in.

"And you have been the one to discover both, Sis. You can't ignore that." Crystal, my only sister, pours margaritas into the salted glasses she's placed in front of Bryce, his husband Nico, me, and Nate. Brad is sipping a Yuengling. My landscaping salt-of-the-earth brother-in-law is not one for any drink that requires salt-rimmed anything.

"What can I say? I attract trouble." I stare at Crystal's plethora of bird feeders and hope that by appearing casual and unperturbed, they'll take the hint and drop the subject.

We're sitting at the antique picnic table that Crystal rescued from our grandmother's farm right before the estate sale after her death. That was over twenty years ago, not long after I'd graduated from the Naval Academy and Bryce had left for London. Without Crystal's quick thinking, we'd be sitting at a mass-manufactured table instead of a family treasure.

Crystal has been the sibling who has kept our roots planted in Stonebridge through the years. She married her college sweetheart, and neither she nor Brad ever thought twice about settling down in central Pennsylvania. With the exception of her time at Lock Haven University, Crystal has remained within five miles of Stonebridge her entire life. She loves to travel, and indeed visited me in each and every duty station I was assigned. She was always quick to point out how much she admired my family's ability to move so much, and confided she'd never be able to leave her birthplace. Crystal's a natural homebody who has taught me a lot about appreciating where I'm from.

"How many for oysters?" Brad asks as he shucks from the other side of the oversized gas grill. The grill's built into the brick wall of their outdoor kitchen and has more burners and gizmos than my brand-new kitchen stove.

We all raise our hands for the ocean delicacy, except Nico.

"You're kidding, right, Nico?" Crystal asks. "You eat octopus, for heaven's sake."

"I ate po-po when I was a kid." Nate keeps a neutral expression. "Where I'm from, in Southern Italy, on the coast, seafood was as typical as PB and Js are here. And like your peanut butter paninis, I outgrew my love of po-po long ago."

"You mean sandwiches, dear," Bryce says in a consoling tone. To Nico's credit, he ignores him.

"I've only ever visited Milan, on business, years ago. Spent a lot of time in Napoli, though." Nate's deep voice rumbles next to me, and I don't mind how the resulting goose bumps remind me that we're in the early days of whatever our relationship turns out to be. Meaning, I'm hopeful we have a lot of time to share in front of us.

"What business was that, again, Nate?" Bryce's inquisitive nature could be defined as nosy, depending on whether you're the one being interrogated by my brother. He's trying a little too hard, if you ask me. Nate doesn't talk about what he did before very much. He's all about today, and the promise of tomorrow. A guy with my kind of attitude. Or at least the attitude I keep trying to adopt.

"Commercial shipping, more or less." A slow smile spreads across his handsome face, and I swallow a giggle. It's killing Bryce that no one seems to really know what Nate did before he became a corporate refugee (his words) and fled to the exotic shores of Stonebridge. I know his past profession, but if Nate doesn't want to share with my family yet, I'm not going say anything, either.

"Logistics?" Brad sets a platter of grilled oysters in the center of the table. We pass around the small appetizer plates, hot sauce, and sliced lemons. With no more preamble, we dig in.

"Don't you want a little taste, hon?" Bryce waves an oyster under Nico's nose. Nico waves him off, pasting that smile back on, but I see the flash of fire in his eyes.

"No, thank you very much, *dear*."

"You don't know what you're missing, dear," Bryce says. He slurps from the shell and Nico grimaces. I bite my lower lip to keep from laughing.

"Not logistics per se, Brad." Nate takes a sip of his margarita. "I was a merchant marine for twenty-five years. Took ships all over the world, until I didn't anymore."

"So you both have a nautical background," Brad muses.

"You didn't go to the Merchant Marine Academy in Kings Point by any chance, did you?"

"Actually, yes, I did."

Exclamations erupt from the crowd, with the obvious comparison made. Both Nate and I are "academy grads," but of different ilk.

"It's like you were meant to meet each other here!" Crystal grins.

"Talk about serendipity, Sis," Bryce says between slurps.

"What made you decide to open a coffee shop in Stonebridge?" Crystal's surprised that I didn't let this juicy tidbit about Nate's shipping background slip during one of our girl chats, I'm sure.

"Like me, Nate wanted a change." I look at Nate. "Sorry, it's not my place to—"

He squeezes my hand. "I like that you feel protective of me," he whispers in my ear before responding to Crystal.

"Angel's right. I wanted a change, something far from what had become a grind for me. I'll always love the sea, and have an affection for it. But after so long, it was time. And full disclosure: I picked a place close enough to my hometown to be able to help out my parents. I grew up in Lancaster and wanted to be here as they age. They're about a decade older than your folks."

"You're a good man," I whisper in his ear and give him a peck on the cheek.

Nate responds with an appreciative gaze and quick

squeeze of my thigh under the floral-print tablecloth. It wasn't easy keeping my mouth shut around my family about his merchant marine career. I was bursting when I found out he'd been a sea captain. Because, as Crystal observed, it certainly does feel as though Nate and me finding one another at this juncture in each of our lives is more than coincidence.

At the risk of sounding a little woo-woo, let me say I'm grateful we both followed our bliss to the same small central Pennsylvanian town.

How I equate bliss with what's quickly becoming killer town is beyond me. Best not to overthink it.

Chapter Seven

THE GROUP FALLS silent, and it takes me a beat to realize they're staring at me. Everyone. Except Nate, who keeps his hand on my thigh, which is very reassuring. And sexy.

"What? Why are you all looking at me as if I'm going to explode or something?"

"You're being unusually quiet," Crystal says.

"That's not true. I just interrupted Nate when you asked him a question and I started to answer it."

"How are you doing, Angel? Really. We're your family. You're safe with us," Nico speaks up.

"I don't know." I look at my brother. "Bryce, how are you doing?" I deflect.

"Are you kidding me? I am trying to forget yesterday afternoon ever happened." He looks over his shoulder. "Brad, anymore oysters, pal?"

"No, but the main course is almost up," Brad replies.

"Stop avoiding the question, both of you. You've both been through a serious trauma," Crystal persists.

"Not as much as poor Hank. To see that dog leash in his

hand was the saddest thing, if you ask me." Bryce's comment isn't a quip but filled with genuine compassion. He and Nico adore their dog, Purl, the yippy but adorable Pomeranian. My heart tugs on my tear ducts and I blink, not wanting to lose it. When Bryce doesn't add more, I decide to talk.

"I thought it was odd that Hank's head was in such an obvious position against the rock. It really looked like he'd hit his head on the way down. As if his dog, Moose, had pulled too hard and Hank slipped. I was shocked when I heard the coroner say 'murder.'" I spear a corncob with Crystal's bright-red glass holders. "Nice cob holders, Sis."

"I got them from the best shop in town." Crystal winks at me. She bought them at Shop 'Round the World.

I grin. While the shop specializes in gifts from around the globe, I've found a plethora of local artisans whose wares I proudly sell. "This particular artist is a genius. Besides the glass corncobs and paperweights, she makes exquisite hand-blown ornaments that I've already ordered for Christmas."

"This early?" Brad sits down, his grilling finished.

"Stop!" Crystal slaps the table with her palm. "I swear, Angel, you are the diversion queen. You're a master of distraction, too, Bryce. For the love of Pete, answer Nico's question."

"I'm fine, really. I mean, sure, I feel sick to my stomach when I think about finding Hank. And poor Verity. I know what she's going through. Not the murder part, but the becoming a widow too young part." I leave out that I think

Hank treated her like a dog. And how the statistic about the spouse being the number one suspect is wafting in and out of my investigative thoughts.

"What aren't you saying, Angel?" Crystal knows me so well, I'm certain she can see my mental cogs churning. Still, I can't talk about all the details. While it's not always spoken, I do have an integrity code with Trinity. I'm not giving away facts about an open case that no one else needs to know. I stick to what's closest to public knowledge.

"Verity and Hank were in my shop earlier yesterday."

"How much earlier?" Bryce asks. I hadn't told him about it, either.

"Right before I left to meet you at the creek." I try to focus on my corn but my appetite is fleeting.

"Wait, so Verity and Hank Price were in your store hours before Hank slipped and fell into the creek?" Crystal's chafing at her bit, turning my reluctance into annoyance.

"Yes, it seems so. Look, we don't know a lot about what's happened, Crystal. It's not your—I mean, my, or our—job to wonder about any of it. Leave it to the police." My voice is grating even to my ears. I'm not very successful at keeping my tone light, noncommittal. I rarely am, in fact.

"Be fair, Angel. We all know you are a brilliant problem solver. That said, we're worried. You got way too involved in the last murder investigation." Nico gets away with what from either of my siblings I'd consider a put-down.

"You mean Frannie." My stomach cringes at the food

that only moments earlier tasted delicious.

"You solved Frannie's murder," Nate says. "And that was incredible. You showed great bravery. But what I think Crystal, and Nico, and all of us are trying to say, I'm sure, is that we care about you and don't want you going through any of that again."

"It's not as if I go hunting for murder victims. Trust me, I don't want to go through anything like that ever again, either. And I know my place, too—I'm not a law enforcement official. But you can't blame me for being upset, for wondering who could do such a heinous act right here in Stonebridge. On Jacob's Run, for Pete's sake." What I leave out is that I was one of the last people to see Hank alive, maybe the last person to see Verity and Hank together while he was still alive. Which is the same situation with Frannie. Besides the murderer, I was probably the last person to speak to her. They'll figure it out if they haven't already.

"No one's blaming you for anything, Angel. But I will blame you if you get yourself shot at again!" Crystal says.

"Fair enough." I take deep breaths, gulp down some water. Nate puts his arm around my shoulder, his warm presence a comfort.

I know what Nate said is true. They all care about me. It's mutual, believe me.

But I care about Stonebridge, too. And my mother's ancient archaeological efforts. I don't want anything threatening it, and that includes whoever killed Hank Price.

AFTER DINNER, CRYSTAL and I watch from the expansive deck as the guys sling horseshoes. We're sitting on her swing, citronella oil ablaze in tiki torches. The light breeze takes care of the lingering humidity.

"Are you really okay, Sis?" Crystal angles toward me, one leg folded in front of her on the swing while she rocks us with the other.

"Surprisingly, I am. And I don't think it's because I've seen dead—murdered—bodies before. Or because I'm trained to handle crises." I'm sitting cross-legged, a cold glass of hibiscus tea in my hands. I passed on an extra glass of wine; I know from my last murder investigation that I'll want a clear mind in the morning.

Just in case. In case Trinity asks me to pitch in, in whatever volunteer capacity I can. In case my brain makes connections I've until now missed. And the worst reason of all: in case the killer strikes again.

"You were thrown by Frannie's murder. What's making the difference now, Sis?" No longer in interrogation mode, Crystal's being the older sister I've always been able to trust with my most fragile emotions.

"First, I've been back home longer. When Frannie was killed, I was still getting used to being out of the Navy and easing back into life as a civilian. Stonebridge was still brand-new to me in many ways. Now, I have a wider safety net, if that makes sense. Of course I know you, Bryce, and Mom and Dad are always here for me. But I've made new friends, remade lifelong friends like Trinity. So as upsetting as it was to find my second murder victim, I know I'm not alone with it. Trinity might have to put Bryce and me on her suspect list as we were the ones who found the body, but she knows me better. I'm not worried about being wrongly accused this time. Does any of this make sense to you?"

Crystal nods. "It does. Go on."

"Second, the store is up and running now, so I don't have the added pressure of trying to launch a business while something so awful is going on. The girls are home to pitch in and Amy's a dependable employee. Third, Hank's death doesn't have anything to do with the shop, nothing to do with me or our family." *But it might involve Mom's pet project, the eel weir.*

"What?" Crystal's doing the mind-meld again.

"Tell me something. Don't you think it's odd that his body was smack-dab in the middle of the weir excavation site?" I ask.

"Yes and no. He had his dog's leash with him, right? Both Brad and I have been dragged by our dogs a time or two, and it's easy to end up in the water if you don't let go soon enough. The creek bank is really steep in several areas, and that spot in particular is messy."

"I know. Dogs love to run into the creek at that spot because of how the water pools after it passes over the weir.

The exception to the rule is Mach."

Crystal laughed. "I still can't get over the fact that Nate named his dog Macchiato. And that you thought it was about the speed of sound!"

"Hey, give me a break. It's a logical link, with my background."

"Speaking of which, have you gone flying lately?"

Regret pushes away my consternation over Hank's death. "No. Not since Mother's Day." I took both Mom and Crystal for a ride in May. Bryce declined the offer, preferring to stay grounded to provide the postflight refreshments.

"That was so much fun. I thought Mom was going to pee her panties when you did that engine stall maneuver."

"You mean she didn't?" We giggle. I still see my mom's expression of terror and delight as we flew up, down, and around the only place she's ever lived.

I've kept my pilot's license active since retiring from the Navy, and get air time as my schedule allows. Stonebridge and all of south central Pennsylvania is beautiful on the ground, but in the skies it lies like a treasure map. The small downtown area is neat and tidy, as if its founder, Jacob Stoner, had a vantage point and made the roads the same way Crystal, Bryce, and I used to, in the backyard sandbox we spent countless hours in. We'd drag the garden hose out to the box and fill our version of Jacob's Creek with an endless supply of water. Until Mom or Dad found us out and ordered us to shut off the faucet.

I enjoy flying all over our area. To the east of town proper is the Susquehanna River and state capital, Harrisburg. I've flown over the Susquehanna several times, marveling at the ever-changing scenery, from farm fields to mountains to deep, mysterious woods.

"Maybe I need to go back up again, sooner than I'd planned. Mom pointed the weir out from altitude. I'd love a second look," I muse aloud. An airplane wouldn't be the best way to check it out, though. But a drone would be perfect, and the twins gave me one for Christmas. The unopened gift is on my closet shelf.

"Hold on, Angel. I hear scheming in your tone. Let me guess. You want to see the crime scene from a different vantage point?"

"What could it hurt?" Mentally I calculate when I'm free to do just that in the next few days. The weather is another factor. Late June's an iffy month thanks to high humidity and frequent late-afternoon thunderstorms. "Although I don't know when I'd have time to. It'd have to be earlier in the day, and I'm too swamped at the shop to take a morning off." Although if it would help solve Hank's murder sooner, it'd be worth whatever extra hours I'd have to work in the evenings and before opening.

"I shouldn't be encouraging you, but isn't that what your employees and daughters are for? To allow you time off?" Crystal stands and stretches, then jumps up and down. "Way to score, Brad!"

Brad wins the round of horseshoes amid mock groans from the other men. Maybe the distraction will allow Crystal to drop her concern over my involvement in the murder investigation, official or not. She turns to face me and her expression's stern again. I know it's silly—Crystal's my sister and I trust her—but I hold my breath, waiting for the zinger I know she's been mentally marinating.

"I know that you're an intelligent woman whose mind needs a challenge. Solving crime, the more complicated the better, is probably a great way for you to beat the boredom everyday small-town life can sometimes foster. But make sure you're minding your p's and q's, Sis. Don't even think of doing anything until you talk to Trinity."

Zap. Right to my conscience.

Chapter Eight

CRYSTAL'S WARNING TUMBLED through my restless sleep last night and I'm eager to rest my weary conscience by talking to Trinity as soon as possible. We usually meet on Monday mornings if only for a few minutes of coffee gabbing, when she's not called away by work. I go downstairs to the shop right after breakfast hoping she'll still show even with Hank's murder on her plate.

Trinity enters the shop at eight o'clock on the dot. If we used analog clocks instead of our phones, that is. Relief relaxes my shoulders.

"*Hiya, pretty lady!*" Ralph greets Trinity as she walks down the small hallway to my back office. He's just outside my office door, on the bird stand that I roll from the back office or storage room to the retail front, depending on where I'm working. Ralph is a yellow-naped Amazon parrot, and his iridescent green feathers and sunny yellow nape have become a Shop 'Round the World trademark. And that's before he opens his beak, more often to talk than bite.

"Good morning, Ralph." Trinity grins.

"*Scratchy, scratchy?*" Ralph bows his head, beak to his

perch, exposing his favorite place to be pet.

"Sure thing, pretty boy." She extends her elegantly manicured fingers to him and gives the parrot the attention he craves. Ralph softly trills as she rubs the tender skin on his nape. It's the parrot version of purring.

"You know you're risking your fingers, right?" I ask.

"Naw. He knows I'm a bird person." Trinity has two lovebirds and has been thinking about rescuing a larger bird.

"He does. Your usual?" I nod at the extensive beverage station I've set up on a custom counter in my office. Expecting to spend long days here, I'm prepared for any beverage craving, from espresso to matcha tea, bamboo whisk included. There are also several bins laden with everything from cinnamon sugar pretzels to tiny chocolate bars to horseradish-flavored potato chips. Pennsylvania's snack food production status—number one in the world—is no joke.

"Hmm, sure. Of course. But do you have any oat milk? I'm taking a break from dairy."

"Did my shop sign change to Latte Love?" I grin. "Just kidding. For you, my dear friend, I have oat milk."

"Thank you." She moves from Ralph and sits down in front of my desk. Trinity is the image of a successful law enforcement officer. She was wooed from the city to the West Shore of the Harrisburg metro area because of her stellar record as first a police officer and then a detective. She's the number two to the Stonebridge chief of police and SPD's senior detective. Her dark-navy dress pants are perfectly pressed, as is her blazer and crisp white shell.

"Aren't you hot in that suit?" I'm already in a sleeveless linen dress and sandals with no intention of wearing anything else today. No air conditioning can keep up with the relentless heat.

"I'm hot no matter what I'm wearing." She flashes a bright grin. "It's a linen blend. And trust me, by the end of the day, I'll want to peel my blazer off. But the gun tends to put the tourists off." Her mouth curves into a wry smile.

"We don't want to scare the tourists. Although, if some of the people in this town have their way, there won't be any reason for tourists to come here."

I'm brewing Trinity's coconut almond latte—I have an assortment of syrups—and a shot of espresso for me as we talk.

Trinity waves her hand at my comment. "Stonebridge, and the surrounding area, will always be a draw for out-of-towners. The people putting up the most fuss are afraid of change is all. In case you need to be reminded."

"No, I don't need the reminder, thank you. Why is it that for as long as we've lived here, it's always been the same group of folks who don't want to see progress?"

Her brow arches at the same time she lets out a sardonic laugh. "You sure you want to ask me that?"

I shake my head. "No. I'm sorry. You understand better than I do how awful some people can be. I'm protective of my mother, and I happen to think that determining whether or not the weir is ancient is important. It's not just about Stonebridge."

"Yeah, well, tell that to the naysayers," Trinity says.

"It would be easier if they formed their own group, in protest of the weir research and excavation."

"Oh, but then we'd have someone to speak to directly. To try to reason with. This way they can continue with the graffiti on public property and sending anonymous letters to the editor about how the Stonebridge Historical Guild is the bane of their life."

I see an opening in our dialogue and I can't hold back. "Do you think the weir project had anything to do with Hank's death, Trinity?"

She takes moment, a thoughtful expression blanketing her face. "No. No, I don't. But I can't rule it out. I'm leaving all options on the table for now."

I hand her the latte and take the guest seat next to hers.

"Meaning you haven't eliminated anyone from your suspect pool? Including Bryce and me."

Trinity nods. "Correct." There's no edge to her tone, no reason for me to believe my brother and I are prime suspects. *Phew.* I wasn't overly worried about it, but as I told Crystal last night, it's wonderful to be where I'm loved.

"I really like our morning meetings, Trinity." I mean it. What I'm really saying is that I'm grateful Trinity and I have reestablished our long-lost best friendship.

"I do, too." She sips her drink.

"Any news on the case?" I've mentioned that finesse isn't always in my social skill set, right?

Trinity looks at her smartwatch, raising her brow in the manner that always makes me laugh. "Two questions in under two minutes. A new record, even for you."

"Can you blame me? I found Hank, after all."

"Repeat after me. I, Angel Warren, am not a law enforcement officer."

"Please." I blow a gold wisp of hair from my eye. "I'm not trying to do your job, honest. It's not like I don't have enough going on with my own life. But you have to admit that my background doesn't hurt when it comes to solving puzzles. And what about all those cold cases that citizens solve? The police are always grateful."

"I forgot for a second that you are indeed the queen of cold case documentaries on television. And if Stonebridge had a pile of cold cases, I'd happily turn them over to you." Trinity sinks farther into the easy chair and puts her feet on the edge of my desk. She takes another sip of the latte. "Mmmm. Does Nate know what a good barista you are?"

I laugh. "Please. It's all about the syrup, you know. Which Nate's been supplying me."

I do my best to sit still, appear relaxed. Trinity's not going to tell me anything unless she very well wants to. And I don't want to give her any reason to think I'm putting pressure on her to spill. It's all I can do to not fidget, to not give her what the girls call my knock-it-off expression. The same look they get from me whenever they're stalling over telling me the truth.

Trinity lets out a long sigh and I tense, praying that my patience is about to be rewarded.

"Okay. Here's the deal." She puts her feet back on the floor and sets her mug at the edge of the natural-edge desk. Her gaze is intent as she looks at me. As if she's about to give me the keys to every murder case ever. "You already heard some of this. You know we were pretty certain Hank was murdered, which is hard to deny with a bullet through his heart."

"Yes."

"Preliminary autopsy results are in. Hank died from the bullet wound."

"By the same bullet found at the scene?"

"Yes. This case is going to be tough nut to crack, though."

"Verity is the prime suspect, no?"

"There was no evidence of gunpowder residue on her or in her home. No weapon or ammunition in the Price house matches the killing bullet."

Well, that shoots my half-formed theory on Verity killing Hank out of the water. So if it wasn't his wife, who could it be? Who would want to kill such an upright member of our community? "There's absolutely no question it was murder?"

"None whatsoever. A shot to his chest cavity with a

hunting cartridge, smack-dab in the middle of off-season. It doesn't get much more deliberate. The only other explanation is if a stray bullet from the firing range got him, and the range is too far away. There are too many obstructions between it and where he fell off the path. The shot that killed Hank was very deliberate."

"Why would anyone want to kill him?" I break eye contact as my gaze wanders. I still see the way Verity jumped when that whistle sounded. What if that was a thin layer, a tiny fraction of how he regularly treated her? Verity's an intelligent woman who'd be more than capable of cleaning up her tracks, evidence-wise.

"You're doing it again, Angel. Letting your thoughts wander where they shouldn't." Her brow arches, emphasizing her large eyes and high cheekbones.

"What do you do with your eyebrows, Trinity? They're always perfect." As I'm entering this new phase of my life—otherwise known as "not as young anymore"—I've discovered my beauty routine needs some updating.

"Stop deflecting. And thank you." Trinity's not in girl-talk mode.

"I thought you forgave me for butting in on Frannie's case," I say.

"More like I let it go." Trinity's mouth is in the same straight line I remember from middle school, the one she wore when she was about to lose it with one of our classmates who'd crossed the line from behaving ignorantly to being a bigot. Trinity is from a white mother and Black father. Thirty years ago, she was one of two Black kids in our entire grade of five hundred. Our school system hosted, and still does, students from all the surrounding small towns and boroughs throughout the county. We've had a modicum of change in the diversity of the population, but it's been extremely slow, too slow.

"You're already mad at me over this case and I haven't done anything yet."

Trinity shakes her head. "I'm not mad at you. I'm not mad at anyone. It's me." She throws her hands up. "I'm frustrated as all get-out. Our department is swamped thanks to the tourist season. I'm working twelve- to fourteen-hour days. I can honestly use your brain power. But as a cop, I can't ask a citizen to volunteer in any way, shape, or form on a homicide investigation."

"But if a citizen were to offer tidbits of information as she uncovers them, that's not against the rules, is it?" I already know the answer.

And both Trinity and I know I'm not going to be able to keep my nose out of this.

"Let's have some ground rules from the start this time," she says.

"Great. I like rules, you know that. Heck, give me some orders." It's all I can do to not break into a happy dance.

"You don't talk to anyone before clearing it with me. You call me whenever you find anything out, ASAP."

"Of course." I really hope I look calm, as if I don't plan to do much more than ask a few questions, maybe walk back over to the crime scene. By the way Trinity's shooting side-eye at me, I'm failing at a detached facade.

"One more thing, Angel."

"Yes?"

"Do not tell anyone anything I ever say to you. You know I trust you as my friend. Implicitly. An active case is different. I have to know I can trust you with sensitive details."

"That's a given. I never repeat a word." Especially if it involves an ongoing homicide investigation.

"Don't make me regret giving in to you, Angel." Her words are direct, no-nonsense. Her gaze sparks with a combination of relief, amusement, and gravity. Murder is no kind of funny business.

"Trinity, I can't thank you enough for your trust. I promise I won't let you down. And you didn't give in to me. I haven't nagged you about this case at all yet." Questioned, sure. But all within casual conversation, right? "Second, do you regret anything about how I helped with Frannie's case?"

"Other than the part where you were shot at by the real killer?" Fire snaps and crackles in the depths of her dark eyes, reminding me that Trinity is a true warrior. Keeping our streets safe so that folks can debate over whether or not we want to know if a pile of rocks is one of the ancient wonders of the world. So that I can enjoy the heavenly scent of Mrs.

Carver's pale-pink roses when I walk my trash out to the back-alley dumpster without having to worry about being mugged. Mostly, to know that there's someone there who cares if I need to dial 9-1-1.

"That was scary but you had my six the entire time." I use the military expression for "covering my ass."

"Thank God." She sighs. "And you kept the killer talking long enough to seal the case. You were stellar, Angel. I don't ever want to see you at the wrong end of a weapon again, though."

"I hear you. And thanks for all you do, Trinity. For being my friend, and for putting up with my inquisitive tendencies."

"No thanks needed, girlfriend. It's my privilege to call you my friend." She stands up and places her empty mug in the small sink near the coffeepot. "I've got to go. Stay safe and keep me informed. No exceptions."

With that she leaves, saying a quick good-bye to Ralph, and heading through the building to exit the store. The bells chime her departure, and Ralph issues his belated farewell.

"Bye bye, hon."

Chapter Nine

WITH TRINITY'S BLESSING—ALBEIT reluctant—I feel as if I've been given a special flight assignment from the airwing commander. Best of all, I no longer need to feel guilty about butting in on the investigation. I have permission, no matter how unofficial my role is.

And do you know what? My family's right. I need this, the crime-solving part of my new life. It's giving me more than the mental challenge everyone seems to think I'll wither without, though. It offers me a way to give back to the community without expectation of compensation or reward of any kind. It's what I did in uniform on a daily basis. And I miss it. I don't have to anymore, because I'm helping catch a very bad person. A murderer.

I have a clear objective. Find Hank's killer. Without screwing up Trinity's *official* investigation.

First things first. I need to find out more about Hank, his daily life, his relationship with Verity. There's always more than what outsiders see, and no matter how opinionated I am, I can't judge Hank, or Hank and Verity's marriage, on one bad scene in my shop.

Verity's the obvious target for questioning, but I can't bother her, not yet. Hank's body hasn't been released by the medical examiner yet. It will be, within the next day or two most likely. It'll allow Verity to finalize whatever funeral or memorial service options she's choosing. I hope to wait until his body is released before I insert myself into her nightmare.

I'm not about to waste time waiting on the coroner's report, though. Trinity gave me the okay and I'm going for it full steam ahead.

This is why I'm on all fours—all threes, actually—with one leg kicked up behind me, my hands firmly planted under my nose, atop my bright-green yoga mat. Our town's premier yoga instructor, Eloise, employs her soothing voice to direct the class through sweaty asanas, or poses. I match my limbs to her cues as best I can. I've been attending her classes pretty regularly since January, but today I have a different motive than aligning my chakras.

I want the dirt on Verity.

Eloise is another one of my high school classmates. Unlike Trinity, Eloise and I were never more than acquaintances but we've become chummier with each class I take, and in seeing one another in town. Her studio is in the building across the street, kitty-corner from mine, so it's beyond convenient.

To be fair, yoga is something I think of as an hour-long stretch for my aching lower back and tight IT band. I've been a runner since high school cross-country. I ran for Navy when I was at Annapolis, and kept up with three-to-five milers a few times each week after graduation. It was the easiest way to stay in top shape for my job as a helo pilot. Now I much prefer a quick walk, or better, a long bike ride.

I have to admit that when I first retired last year, I was a little off-kilter in terms of exercise. Without regular fitness tests to worry about and a booming new business, it was easy to let a day's work out go here and there. Until my favorite jeans got tight and I figured it was time to get at it again. Running isn't enough, though, nor is biking or other cardio that I enjoy. I need to give my body more varied activity. Geesh, I sound like I'm...not twenty-five anymore. My groan is stifled by moving back into a seated position, where Eloise tells us to check in with our body again and to notice where it's changed during the practice.

"Thank you for sharing your practice with us." She bows her head.

Just like that, Eloise ends the class and I'm ready to go back to work. I need the Zen mind to tackle my back storage room while Amy works retail. After I get some answers, of course.

I wait until the class clears before I approach Eloise at her desk.

"Great class, Eloise. Thank you."

She smiles, her wide eyes full of serenity under her purple headband, which coordinates perfectly with her pansy-print yellow tank top and violet leggings. "It's nice to see you,

Angel. Been busy at the shop, I take it?"

"Yes. It's no excuse for not sticking to my routine, though." I'm not a humid weather yoga girl, to be honest. I like the classes to warm up in during the colder months when it's too icy to walk or run.

"We're not getting younger. It's important to learn to take time for ourselves now." She doesn't add "before we're too wizened to" but I get the gist.

"You're right. I should be in here more." I really mean it. My legs feel a gazillion times looser than when I walked in. "Do you have some time to talk?"

"To you? Always!"

"I appreciate it. You might have some insight I need at the moment. Please tell me if I overstep."

"This sounds suspiciously like last year, when you came in to talk about Frannie. I heard that you were the one who found Hank Price." Her gaze softens. "You've been attracting some serious low energy since you moved back. Why don't you let me come over to the shop after hours? I'll clear the space for you. I just received a new batch of herbs."

"Uh, okay, let's do that sometime." Eloise is a gifted yoga instructor and isn't afraid to embrace the entire spectrum of yogic and spiritual tools handed down through the ages. I could do with keeping a more open mind, no question. Yet I'm more of a rule or list person. I like definite boundaries. Clearing a space with smoking herbs is more of a blurry proposition for me.

"What do you need to know, Angel?" she asks.

"It's something sensitive. I know you're friends with Verity Price, and they were both in my store a few hours before Hank's death." I watch her reaction. I don't want to push her no matter how badly I want the goods on the Prices. She's in pain from the loss, too.

Eloise nods. "It's been horrific. For all concerned, but mostly for Verity. Can you imagine, your husband goes out for a walk but never comes back?"

Actually, I can, except in my case Tom died of an awful cancer, and we had time to say good-bye. "I know what it's like to lose a spouse, but not so abruptly, no."

"Of course you do." Eloise places her hand on my forearm for a few seconds. Enough to convey that she's heard me when we've discussed the years leading up to my return to town. "So I'm sure you understand that Verity's still in shock. The funeral planning, the financials—" She stops short.

"Financials? I mean, I know funerals are expensive. But they have a very successful business, right?"

"Times have been tough, you know. I realize that since you moved back last year, Stonebridge has been booming. It wasn't always so busy downtown, though. There was the recession almost fifteen years ago, and another long time span where all the businesses were closing because of retirements or deaths. We had a long spell of slow sales, no new businesses opening. It's taken years of patience, investment, and sacrifice for Stonebridge to come back to life."

"Price Chiropractic hasn't been here that long, though, has it?"

"No, you're right. They opened their office no more than eight, maybe ten years ago." A thoughtful expression intensifies the few lines on her face. Eloise stands up. "I'm getting a cup of tea. Would you like one?"

"I'll never turn down a cup of your matcha." Don't tell Nate, but Eloise has the best matcha tea in town. Latte Love is a great coffee place, and has a nice assortment of loose-leaf teas. I happen to prefer my green tea with some powder, which Eloise is sprinkling on top of the steaming liquid.

As we settle into the comfortable chairs around her desk, hot ceramic tea bowls in hand, I can't help thinking about how Eloise helped me out last year, when I was investigating—though I insisted at the time I was merely inquiring about—Frannie's murder. The reality of two murders in my hometown gut punches me again, and I rest the warm pottery against my midsection.

Eloise's eyes narrow. "You're protecting your relationship chakra, Angel."

"Am I?"

"Yes. It's a golden yellow, right over your liver. Yours is tinged with a burnt-orange shade, sprinkled with amber. Is it Nate? Trouble in paradise already?" she asks in that quiet way of hers that never comes off as nosy or rude. As I'm certain I do at times. Or often. Maybe most of the time.

"No, no, Nate and I are well. Our relationship is getting better all the time, in fact. I mean, it's still early days, but so far it's as though we've always known one another. Does that sound odd?" I inwardly cringe. Yes, I realize that tit for tat is needed when asking for intimate details about someone. Sharing my personal life outside of my inner circle isn't something I'm used to doing, though.

"That doesn't sound odd at all. Soul mates are just that. Someone you've traveled with before." Eloise doesn't look or act as "out there" as she sounds, trust me. And I don't pooh-pooh any of her theories. I certainly have my share of personal woo-woo; much of it's leftover from being a pilot. The navy and sailors in particular have a long history of superstitious ritual. Add in my Catholic upbringing with a cast of saints to implore for spiritual support, and I have my own syllabus of spiritual extracurriculars.

"Nate's exactly who I needed at this point in my life, no question. I never would have thought I'd find someone again, at least not someone I could…" Oh geez, do I want to expose my most vulnerable parts to Eloise? She's not my sister or Trinity, my two most trusted confidantes. Or my girls, who I'm as close to as I suppose a mother can be to nineteen-year-old adolescent women.

"Spend the rest of your life with?" Eloise prompts.

"Yes. But we're not at that stage. Yet." I need to stretch myself past how closely I guard my private thoughts a bit here. "Can I, do I, see the possibility of a more permanent future with Nate? Absolutely." It's a risk to say it aloud but from the immediate sense of relief I feel—yes, in my yellow chakra region—I know I can trust Eloise.

"That's the best part about getting to our stage of the game, isn't it? We know what works and what doesn't, and if we're smart, do the spiritual footwork, we can make better choices than we would have, say, twenty years ago."

"You're right. In that vein, what's going on with Verity? You mention financials. Only if you're comfortable sharing, of course." I squirm at how easily I make asking for gossip sound altruistic.

The barely perceptible lines on Eloise's forehead knit. "I was going to send out a group text to our Stonebridge High ladies as so many of us are her patients. Verity may need help for the funeral expenses. I was thinking about launching a fundraising page for her. Of course I wouldn't make it open to the entire public. It'd be a private fundraiser among us." She refers to a group of ten or twelve of us who graduated Stonebridge High together and have stayed in touch. I didn't stay in touch as well as the others, but they looped me in on their emails and texts after word got around that I'd helped to solve Frannie's murder. They often do works of charity like chipping in for an event that a Stonebridge citizen can't otherwise afford, or making sure an elderly neighbor gets their winter fuel bills paid.

"That's very nice of you. Maybe we just need to take up a quiet collection between us?"

"Maybe, for the funeral." Eloise shakes her head. "None of us have enough to help her out of the hole she's in. Verity's circumstances are dire, I'm afraid."

"Everyone raves about her clinical ability, and I've never driven past her office and not seen a full parking lot. How can she be short on funds?"

"Verity is—was—only half of the business."

"You mean Hank wasn't doing as well? I'd think her half of the business would more than make up for his shortfalls." Thinking about it, I discover that I don't know anyone who uses Hank as their chiropractor. The praise I hear on the street is always about Verity.

"You really don't know what happened, do you?" Eloise asks.

"Don't forget, as you said, I've only been back a year." Funny how time works. It often feels like my twenty-plus years of military service was a dream, that I've never left central Pennsylvania.

"Right." She sighs, takes a long sip of tea. When she refocuses on me, her eyes are bright.

"The short version is that Hank hasn't laid a hand on a single patient in the entire time they've lived here and had their practice. Verity handles all adjustments and chiropractic services. Along with the new chiropractor they hired last month."

"I didn't realize there was new person on staff. So what does Hank do? Sorry. I mean, what did Hank do at the practice, exactly?" I cringe at my slipup. I'm the last one who should forget he's dead, as I'm the one who discovered his body floating in Jacob's Run, for heaven's sake.

"Hank was the numbers guy. He handled the books, all the promo, anything other than patient care."

"But he's a chiropractor, too, right?" Maybe I've been mistaken in my assumption that they were both chiropractors. They certainly gave that impression at the Stonebridge Buddies meetings.

"Yes, you're correct, Hank was a chiropractor. It seems that after they married, it became clear, for whatever reasons, that Verity was better at adjusting spines while Hank was a brilliant financier, a natural at running a business." Eloise lowers her voice, even though we're the only two in the building between her classes. "Or so we thought. According to Verity, all of their accounts save one have been drained. Unbeknown to her, Hank pulled out a huge chunk of funds only one week before he died."

"Where did the money go? Do you have any idea?" Maybe they paid off that beautiful home I've only ever seen from the street.

"That's just it. Verity doesn't know, or if she has any idea, she's not saying. Verity and I have been good friends for at least the last five years. We met in her office as I'm one of her patients. We talk through my adjustments, and when she found out I was a yoga instructor, that was it. We're soul mates, of a sort. She's the little sister I never had."

"This must be awful for you, too, Eloise. I'm so sorry." I am in that questionable place that's beyond uncomfortable. In the navy most things fell down on one side or the other of good versus bad, honest versus dishonest, straightforward versus manipulative. When I was preflighting my aircraft, there was no middle ground. Either the helicopter was in good enough shape to fly, or it needed maintenance.

This is the second time in a year I've been put in the position where my curiosity wars with my sense of common decency. If Eloise is that tight with Verity, then she's grieving, too. And while I'm insatiable for facts and background on Hank Price, I'm definitely taking advantage of Eloise's fragile state. Except she doesn't look fragile at all.

You want to solve the murder, don't you?

"It's all still a shock. At least for Verity. There's no way she can see past this ugly part, but as her friend I'm angrier at Hank than I've ever been," Eloise says.

"Why did he make you angry?" I ask.

"He ran the show. I felt he didn't give Verity enough credit at times. Verity fell in love with him when she was only twenty-five, over a long weekend, while at her sister's destination wedding in Ravello. It's a seaside resort in Italy."

"I know it well. We were stationed twenty minutes from there, for three years." Memories of hot summer days, warm nights, sipping red wine as the kids polished off their personal plate-sized pizzas do the tarantella across my mind. Tom's smile as we watched the New Year's fireworks from our casa's terra-cotta-tiled rooftop, the sparkling blooms bright against the dark sky. Happy memories that only cause melancholy that the girls are now young women. That horrible sadness over losing Tom has faded into gratitude. I'll forever cherish the time we had, and never not believe it was too short. But I've healed, the twins are having a blast in college, and we have a new, permanent home base in Stonebridge.

"Oh wow, I didn't know that," Eloise says.

"I can understand how Verity fell in love in Ravello. It's pretty close to impossible not to!"

"Maybe I should convince Fred to take me, hmm?" Eloise asks.

"Definitely."

"Well, Verity fell in love, and Hank convinced her to marry him soon after. It seemed perfect, she's always said. Both of them being chiropractors, at the same wedding in Italy? And he's from Baltimore, so not a long way from here."

"How old was Hank?" I remembered the smattering of gray at his temples.

"Ten years older than Verity. And he was in charge of both their relationship and the business, right from the start, from what she's told me. Although, to be fair, Verity didn't put it that way. She said he had the vision that she lacked, and that she was more than happy to let him figure out the direction of their business while she focused on treating patients. It was such a great division of interests for them that Hank turned all of his patients over to Verity. Verity's one of those health providers that's a true healer. It's her calling. I can see why balancing the books never appealed to her."

"I assume he left his practice in Maryland, but when he came here you're saying he became a business manager and not a practitioner?"

"I don't know all of the details, but Verity already had a strong practice here. With her entire family in the area, moving wasn't one of her desirables. Hank said that it wasn't a choice at all for him. The decision for him to pick up and move was made the second he laid eyes on Verity. And while he initially thought he'd practice on patients, too, it wasn't an easy start as no one knew him here and everyone asked for Verity. So he decided he'd be the business manager."

"You've heard him say this?"

"Many times. At dinners, backyard parties, the Stone-bridge Buddies meetings. That's mostly where I've ever spent time with him. It always struck me, how open Hank was about his love for Verity. He was a real charmer, that Hank. Except when he was being a patronizing jerk to Verity, which honestly wasn't often. I don't want you to think he was horrible. I just had some issues with his delivery, let's say."

Doubt weaves into my memory of how snide Hank's comments were to Verity on Saturday. Was it possible I'd seen his absolute worst, that they were having nothing more than a bickering match?

"Thanks for sharing all of this with me, Eloise. It's helping me get a fuller picture."

"You're brilliant and intuitive," Eloise says. "I didn't say anything you wouldn't put together on your own soon enough."

"Thank you for that. I've got to get back to work, but whatever you need for Verity, let me know."

"I will." Eloise and I hug, and the warmth of being welcome in my hometown wraps around me. I need all the extra love I can get after finding Hank dead.

The local funeral parlor is expert at guiding the bereaved of all budget abilities through their final good-byes. Trinity told me that they give deep discounts in extraordinary circumstances, so I think Verity will be okay as far as burial expenses go. If Verity's indeed in the kind of financial straits Eloise is hinting at, there will be plenty of other opportunities to help her out.

As I exit the yoga studio and walk down Main Street, I experience a bolt of gratitude for my life, my family. For Nate. Verity has cruelly lost her biggest ally.

The best action I can take for Verity, and the entire town, is to help Trinity get to the bottom of this sooner than later.

I need to find Hank's killer.

Chapter Ten

I CALL TRINITY the minute I'm out of the shower after the extended yoga session.

"Please tell me you've found out something of value to the case and not another body." Trinity must be somewhere other than at work because she doesn't answer with her usual identification.

"Not a body, but I've gleaned some information you might be able to use." I summarize what Eloise gave up. "There's something fishy with the Prices' finances, if two successful chiropractors haven't made enough to pay for Hank's funeral. You've been here longer than I have, what do you make of it? Is Eloise on point or is it more town gossip?"

"Your biggest cold brew with a dash of cream, please," Trin says.

"What?"

"Sorry, doing the drive-through. I'm on my way to the station."

"You'd better be or I'll tell Nate you're cheating on Latte Love."

"Trust me, I'd love nothing more than to discuss this with you over Nate's coffee in an air-conditioned space. But it isn't happening today. Give me a sec, Angel." I wait as I hear Trinity pay the cashier.

"Mmm that hits the spot," she says.

"Did I hear you order an extra-big cold brew? Do you need to stay up for the next twenty-four hours? That much caffeine would have me flying higher than Ralph, if I didn't keep his wings clipped."

"Caffeine doesn't bother me much. And for the love of Pete, let that poor bird's wings grow in." Trinity has a pair of lovebirds and she's all about free-range flight.

"If I could keep him in a full-size atrium, which is what you've done for Malcolm and Harriet, I would. I have to keep his trimmed for safety's sake. Do you know how many parrots die from indoor flight injuries, or escape, unable to fly home?"

"No, and I'll bet you don't, either."

"Caught." We both laugh. "Look, I can talk to you later. You shouldn't be driving and drinking." My mama bear instincts have never left me after raising the girls.

"I'm in the parking lot. Look, I think you might be onto something here. As a law enforcement officer, I have to caution you against involving yourself with anything that gets dangerous. I trust you to know where the line is."

"And as my friend?"

Her groan is epic. "As your friend, I don't want you

coming face-to-face with a cold-blooded killer if you don't have to."

"I thought you were looking at the possibility of Hank's being accidental." I know I risk pushing Trinity too far—even though she'd given me the green light to investigate—but pushy is in my DNA.

"It's my job to look at all angles, yes. And while it could still end up being a freak of nature or physics, I'm highly doubtful."

"Go on." I place the phone on speaker and start getting dressed. Depending upon what Trinity tells me, I might have good reason to go back out again before dinner, instead of catching up on paperwork with Ralph at my side until Nate stops in for dinner. Weeknight family dinner with the girls has become our summer mainstay since the twins have returned from college.

"There are cases of stray bullets hitting and ricocheting off objects in exactly the right place at exactly the right time to unfortunately hit a person. I wanted to believe that's what happened here, but again, it's my job to stay open-minded."

"Right." Not unlike the navy, law enforcement requires a complete commitment to the effort and a total noncommitment to the various theories and possibilities until all the facts are on the table.

"It's a bridge too far with Hank, Angel. Too many obstructions, as far as I can tell. Buildings, trees, the water…"

"So it's definitely not from the firing range?"

"The range wasn't shooting then," Trinity confirms.

"That's what I thought. I didn't hear a single shot when we were on the creek, just some random firework. I mean, I'm certain it was a firecracker and Bryce agreed with me. I think I'd know the difference between a firecracker and gunshot." Sound travels over water in a way it often doesn't on land. Maybe I heard what I wanted to hear?

"Unless someone was hunting, which means poaching since it's not open season. This was a deliberate act. Hunters usually come forward in my experience." Trinity's in full-on detective mode, her words coming out in clipped perfection. "Which is why I want you to be very, very careful, my friend."

Phew. She's not telling me to stop my investigation. "You know I am."

"Uh-huh." Trinity's sigh is as long as I sense her patience isn't. "The deal here is that you tell me everything you find out, as soon as you find it out. You don't go into any situation that's sketchy. I don't have to define *sketchy* for you, do I?"

"No, ma'am." I do a little jig in front of my mirror.

"Okay, I gotta go," she says.

"Trin?"

"Yeah?"

"Thank you. For your trust."

"Uh-huh."

I've no doubt of her faith in me, but Trinity's go-ahead

can be withdrawn at her discretion. I'd be smart to keep this in mind if I'm tempted to go off script. Oh, who am I kidding? *When* I go off on my own tangent.

I NEED LUNCH so I head to the kitchen, where I hear the girls talking. I don't have to go back to the shop this afternoon as Ava and Lily will take a two-hour shift after Amy's done.

"Mom, Ava and I have been thinking." My twins watch me; Ava's leaning against the counter and Lily's at the kitchen table, Ralph ensconced on her shoulder. Ralph misses the girls so much that when they're around I don't get as much one-on-one with him, other than in the early mornings before they awaken.

"That sounds dangerous." When I don't get as much as a giggle or an eye roll from either of them, I pause. "What is it?"

"We think you should spend more time with Nate," Ava says, shooting her sister a mysterious look.

"Wow, not what I was expecting." I thought they'd overheard my conversation with Trinity and were going to tell me to back off the sleuthing. "What brings this up?"

"You are happy with him, he's happy with you, and being busy with Nate means you have less time to get into trouble," Lily says as she absentmindedly rubs Ralph's beak.

"*Trouble* isn't the word. We mean that we want you to be safe." Ava assumes her eldest sister role, even if it's only by six minutes.

"Does this have anything to do with Hank Price's death?"

"No," they reply in unison, too quickly.

"We, I mean..." Lily trails off.

"What Lily's trying to say is that it's not so much that Hank Price is dead, but that you found him."

"Right," Lily chimes in. "Mom, face it. What are the odds there would be a murder in Stonebridge, and not only is this the second one, you've found both victims all on your own!"

"You have to admit it seems way too odd to be coincidental." Ava sets her coffee mug down and folds her arms over her chest.

"Girls. Let me get my lunch together and then we'll talk."

Lily eyes the kitchen clock. "I have to be in the store in fifteen minutes."

"It won't take that long." I fill a large bowl with the salad mix left over from dinner last night, bleu cheese dressing, and a hunk of chicken breast. Placing the items on the table, I sit at the far end from Lily, with Ava in my line of sight. "Okay, talk."

"We said what we're concerned about. You're our only parent left, and we don't want you getting hurt." Ava's words are practiced, and I wonder how late the two of them were up last night, figuring out how to approach me.

"Or worse," Lily murmurs.

"Girls." I shake the dressing bottle, open it, pour. "I'm not running into these bodies on purpose. They are two unfortunate events, both of which I have nothing to do with, except as you pointed out, I found the deceased."

"Which is enough scary stuff for a lifetime!" Lily's more adamant.

"Let's go after the elephant, shall we?" I ask.

"One bite at a time, we know." Ava's grumbles tickle my funny bone.

"I'm sorry sweethearts, I don't mean to sound patronizing. I'm touched that you care so much. And can we all agree that it's easy for any one of us to 'go there' after what we went through with your father? Losing a loved one is never easy, and you both were so young."

"Dad was young."

"Yes, he was. Too young. And it wasn't that long ago, although I know for you both it probably feels longer. Six years is a third of your lives. I get it."

"Honestly, Mom? It feels a lot more recent to me." Ava's lower lip juts out.

"Me, too." Lily's lip trembles, and I'm dumbfounded. None of us get this emotional so quickly over Tom anymore. The first couple of years after Tom died, heck yeah. It was a crap shoot as to which one—or all—of us would break into waterfalls at what could seem like benign things. Grief was always there, at the surface, waiting to be triggered into total sorrow.

But now, we're almost six years out—

"Oh, I forgot! Tomorrow is the anniversary, isn't it?" I stare at my daughters, my heart breaking open. Not all the way, but enough to feel the pain again.

Ava nods and Lily sniffs.

"Awwww, pretty boy." Ralph's plaintive words are uttered in the most forlorn tone I've ever heard from him. All three of us look at each other, tears freely spilling down six cheeks.

"That's why you're upset." And why Tom's been on my mind more. "Not that thinking about your father's passing shouldn't upset you, but on an anniversary, it's the worst." I get up and pour myself iced tea. "Does anyone else want some?"

"No, Mom. What we want is for you to stop changing the subject," Ava says, wiping her face.

"Yeah, stop trying to distract us." Lily fortifies her sister's stance.

"Okay, okay." I sit back down. "Tell me what you want. And don't distract me with Nate."

They both have the decency to appear mollified, their sheepish expressions not that far off from how they appeared after getting caught lying about whose house they were playing at, when the group of tweens were all going elsewhere.

"We don't want to lose you, Mom. We're scared." Ava's declaration was Lily's cue to put Ralph on his perch stand. Both girls came to me and we had a long group hug.

"You're not losing me. Look, you know me. Remember that big helicopter I used to fly? The one you said looked like it couldn't get off the ground?" As I spoke I wished it'd be as easy as when they were kids to convince them I was capable of anything. There's nothing to replace those fleeting moments when your children look at you as if you're a superhero.

"Yes, Mom. But this isn't a navy op. It's murder, in this town that's supposed to be quiet and safe. There's a shooter out there."

"How did you find that out?" I ask.

"Elijah." They say Trinity's youngest son's name in unison.

"You saw him when?"

"We're on a text chain," Lily explains. "He told us last night."

"You're texting with Elijah? Reggie, too?" I ask. Reggie is Trinity's eldest and a year ahead of my girls. Elijah is about to go off to college in August.

"We're texting one another more for you and Trinity than ourselves," Lily defends.

"It's to stay in the loop on what you two are up to." Ava shrugs. "Nothing you need to know about, honestly." She glares at Lily, who promptly screws up her face at her sister.

"Just keep anything you hear quiet, okay? Until it gets into the paper or on the news, assume it's confidential."

"We don't watch TV news or read the local paper, Mom," Lily says.

"Right. Of course you don't." They hadn't grown up on color print Sunday morning cartoons, or waited for the news to finish so that the Friday night shows could begin.

"We'll keep it on the down-low, Mom," Ava says.

"I know you will. That reminds me. I want us back to Naples rules." We were stationed in Naples—*Napoli*—Italy, for two years. It's our favorite tour to reminisce over, and we adored the local culture. But it was a challenge to not become targets of petty theft in the incredibly cosmopolitan Mediterranean port city. "Naples rules" is our family's code for being cautious. "Check in via text or voice mail every time you change locations."

They groan in unison.

"Worry for each other goes both ways, girls," I say.

We enjoy lunch together, and I marvel at how lucky I am, with this new life I've found. Which makes me all the more determined to do my part to catch the killer. No one makes my girls worry about me.

Chapter Eleven

B Y TUESDAY I'VE waited as long as I can. It's time for more answers. I wrap up a small sympathy gift for Verity, tell Amy I'll be back in the afternoon, and head for the Price residence. I wish I had the larger lantern she's waiting on to bring along, but according to the Middletown distribution center it's not due until later this week. Frankly, I doubt she's concerned about it. She's in that deep place no spouse ever wants to visit.

I don't call ahead as I don't want to chance it that she'll tell me not to come over, which is what I did right after Tom died. I didn't want to see anyone those first several days. Verity might not even be home, but it's worth a shot. Although I can't imagine she'd be back to work at her practice yet. The coroner still hasn't released the body for Hank's funeral.

The Prices' home is something to behold. I've never seen it except from my car as I drive by on my way to Crystal's place, which is out in the farm fields that surround Stonebridge. The Prices' house is set back from the winding road, amid a heavily wooded area that's in fact carefully pruned and landscaped to appear natural. A long drive leads to the woods, and it takes several seconds to drive through the assortment of Bradford pear, evergreen, oak, and maple trees. There are no Tree of Heaven trees to be found on the Price property. I know this because my brother-in-law is their landscaper, and I asked him a few questions about it on the phone earlier, unbeknown to Crystal. Brad will keep my confidence; he knows how obsessive Crystal can be about my safety. It's an older sister thing.

The private road bursts through the forest and into a quiet setting with the ginger brick house demanding immediate attention. I park in the circular drive and get out, bringing her gift with me. I've brought a smaller version of the Japanese lantern that Verity ordered with her Christmas gift certificate. By "smaller," this lantern weighs fifteen pounds instead of over two hundred pounds like the actual, garden-size statuary she's bought. This sympathy lantern is a token of hope for brighter days in the future, my way of trying to bring a little light into such a dark time.

Who am I kidding? I've done everything I can to encourage her to let me in, and not just into the house. The creepy crawlies in my belly remind me again that I'm not anywhere close to being a professional sleuth. My suspicion wars with my compassion. Unlike Trinity, guilt plagues me every time I need to weasel my way into someone's life for the sole purpose of getting information. While Trinity made it clear there's no evidence against Verity, she's still my prime suspect.

Thinking of Trinity reminds me that I didn't tell her I was headed out here. I have to remember that Trinity's allowing me to nose around is a privilege. I don't want her to shut me out of the investigation so I place the gift on my car hood and quickly text her. I'm nosy and manipulative but I won't add disobeying an order from my bestie to my list of sins.

Me: *Stopping at the Prices' to drop a sympathy gift off for Verity.*

Trinity: *Careful.*

Me: *Always.*

I take in the Prices' extensive landscaping, from the perennial beds that line the drive to the supersized hanging baskets on the covered porch. Bright-pink, yellow, and white wave petunias fall in elegant cascades. The white double front doors are framed by topiaries not of the typical boxwood but of burning bush, a native Pennsylvania shrub with bright-green foliage that turns bright crimson in the autumn. A large bench sits to the right of the doors, and two sturdy rocking chairs are to the left. All three pieces of furniture are laden with cellophane-covered baskets and potted plants. Maybe my gift will end up in the pile, too, but I'm hopeful Verity will answer the door.

My positive attitude wanes after three presses of the mother-of-pearl doorbell button. As I turn to leave, I hear a dog's barking echo from somewhere either inside or on the other side of the house. I can't tell which it is. The barking turns into a long howl at the same instant a slight breeze makes the burning bush's leaves tremble. Shivers race across my nape. *Verity isn't in danger, is she? Has her dog been shoved into a room by an intruder?*

Immediately I see the mental image of Verity's corpse, her canine companion wailing his grief next to her.

Stop it. I'm still on overdrive after the creek float with Bryce, and finding Hank.

Verity is probably out back, playing with her dog. I know I spent hour upon hour with Ralph after Tom died. And the last thing I wanted was anyone but my family and a few dearest friends around me. Certainly not an acquaintance, which is all I am to Verity.

I can leave my gift on the bench with the others, drive away, leave Verity in peace. There will be time to question her later. Except—as Trinity has expressed over one of our morning coffee talks—when it comes to solving a murder, time is of the essence. The longer a crime goes unsolved, the less chance of catching the crook. Which in this case is a cold-blooded murderer. Like Trinity, I find it doubtful that someone who shot Hank like that did it by accident. It's not hunting season, and even if it was, a direct hit to his heart while on a secluded part of the creek bed path doesn't add up to accident.

My fingers wrinkle the gift wrap as I clutch the heavy

gift, my raison d'être. I'm not ready to give up yet. I want answers that only Verity can provide. Examining the wide porch, I note a paved path that begins where the porch ends. Grasping the heavy gift bag by the bottom, I follow the walkway around the house, swatting away what little remains of my common decency. It's not trespassing if I didn't see a sign, is it? Plus, it's more polite to leave such a heavy, bulky item closer to where Verity might want to place it. It's as good a reason for busting in on a grieving widow as any, I suppose.

The path turns right and the full expanse of the house is revealed. I walk alongside the length of it, at least one hundred feet, before it curves into a beautifully landscaped perennial garden. Sculptures sit among echinacea and columbine, including a full-breasted mermaid and Pan. The juxtaposition of the art amid the bucolic south central Pennsylvania setting isn't lost on me. I can't say I've ever seen a statue of the half man, half goat in a lot of places besides Europe, and definitely not in an American suburb.

I walk through an arbor of pale-pink roses that rival Mrs. Carver's and into a parcel of property that's invisible from the front of the house. In fact, this sprawling landscape is hidden from the world.

I'm surprised I haven't noticed the Prices' property on one of my flights. Or if I did, I didn't realize it was their place.

I need to get that drone out of its box ASAP.

I like to cruise over Stonebridge and Jacob's Run, using the water as my guide back to our tiny airport. Besides the rolling hills and many tributaries, I've spotted myriad housing developments in various stages of construction. None of them remotely resemble what Hank and Verity have built.

Stonebridge has had an explosion in population growth over the past five years, thus the construction boom. The newest builds in Stonebridge are part of larger developments with anywhere from thirty to fifty homes. The tiny lots are up against each other, with no room for any pretense of countryside. Full fields and stretches of woods are plowed over to put up cluster after cluster of cookie-cutter homes, many of them referred to as "patio" or "garden" homes.

The girls and I moved here at a time when it was financially unfeasible for me to outright purchase one of the new construction homes. Plus I had my business to consider. I'd thought I'd have to buy two properties, but when I saw my building, it was love at first sight.

Purchasing the building I both live and work in was the best decision I've made regarding moving back. Not having an actual yard or garden to worry about is a huge relief for me. Sure, I enjoy puttering with the many different ceramic pots and objets d'art I've collected across the globe. On my balcony. It helps that Crystal, the true green thumb of our family, brings over the prettiest plants and flowers, all ready to pop into said containers. But mowing a lawn, pulling weeds? No, thank you. I'd rather be working in my shop or flying.

It's bothering me that I haven't noticed this portion of land from the air. Which makes me think that flying over Jacob's Run in a plane won't give me the views I need for the investigation. Yeah, it's definitely time to use the Christmas gift from the girls.

The view back here is spectacular. The lawn sprawls out to a gated pool area, and I'll bet the black fence surrounding the manmade oasis is custom wrought iron, not the prefab lengths Brad keeps in stock. I've never seen such ornate prefab fencing, at any rate. As I study the swirls of metal, I realize they're in the shape of a human spine.

The barking increases in volume followed by sounds of splashing. The pool's fence is bordered by rosebushes, all in varied shades of pink, from pale rose to lipstick fuchsia. There's a very pink theme going on with the landscaping. Verity's touch, I'd guess.

The Prices' yard and gardens are well kept, just as I'd expect from a property my brother-in-law manages. The beauty goes beyond good pruning and regular organic lawn treatments, though. The vibrant palette portrayed in the assortment of flora and fauna is stunning. It's like a dream paradise.

Guilt still shadows my manners but I've already crossed the line of respecting someone's privacy.

"Hello!" I try for cheery. I want to talk to Verity, not

scare her to death.

I walk up to the closed gate.

"What?" She sounds surprised.

"Woof!" The soaking-wet Lab covers the distance between the edge of the pool and the fence in one second flat.

I'm in a face-off with a one-hundred-pound dog who doesn't seem to remember ever meeting me.

Chapter Twelve

"MOOSE!" VERITY REPRIMANDS her dog, who immediately sits, his gaze never leaving me. Trinity had reassured me that Moose was safely back home, but it's still wonderful to see the happy doggie in person.

"Angel! From the gift shop. Is my lantern in?" She jumps up from the chaise lounge, throwing a glossy magazine onto a side table. It flaps closed and the sunshiny cover of *Your Garden, Your Way* is a perfect match for the customer I know, but seems odd for a grieving widow.

"Um, no not yet. Verity, I'm so sorry! I didn't mean to intrude like this. I saw the pile of gifts on your porch, and when no one answered I was all set to leave this there. But then I heard Moose, so I thought you might be around. I wanted to make sure everything's okay. I will leave this here and go right back out, promise."

"No, no, that's fine. Moose is a big teddy bear. He won't hurt you, promise. You remember Angel from the store, don't you, Moose?" She opens the gate, which has a top-pull contraption, the kind to keep young children from getting into the pool. "Please, come sit for a minute. Do you want anything to drink?"

"No, thank you." I follow her back to the other side of the pool and notice that the view of rolling green hills yields to large, branchy trees that bend in a graceful arch. "Wow, is that Jacob's Run?"

"Yes. Isn't the view fab? We were so lucky when we found the property. There were two run-down cabins out here, and brambles had invested the entire three acres surrounding them. We bought it all and got to work. It took three months to clear the weeds. I didn't want any of the natural growth hurt if it didn't have to be, so it was slow going."

She's a bit breathless, and I'm not sure if it's due to my surprise drop-in or because she's so enthused to describe her home.

"I had no idea you backed right up to the water." I should, I suppose, being a town native, but I grew up outside of the town proper, in an older, established subdivision. And while I've flown over Stonebridge several times, I'm still getting my land bearings on the area, which is quite different from a bird's-eye view.

"Most people don't realize how close we are to the creek. When we first married, before we owned the property, we'd bring our kayaks to the banks over there, under the willows"—she points—"and have the best picnics." Her mouth curves wistfully under her huge sunhat and dark shades. As if she's remembering all of the things she and Hank did back then, never conceiving it would end so abruptly years later. Perspiration trickles down my back, but I suspect it's from my nervousness more than the relentless sunshine. Not to mention my self-recrimination. Verity's husband has been murdered, and I'm judging her by the magazine she's paging through.

"I am so very sorry, Verity." I place the gift on the glass table that's under its own bright-yellow umbrella. "I brought a little something to let you know I care. And I understand. I lost my husband six years ago."

"Oh, I had no idea!" She removes her shades, makes eye contact. The circles under her swollen lids are the kind bouts of intense sobbing deliver. Compassion squeezes out any hope for me to maintain professional detachment.

"It was a long while ago now, while I was still in the navy. Long before I ever knew I'd be retiring here."

"I knew you'd served. Thank you for your service. I've heard you've been in every country in the world." Her words are hollow, spoken more from habit than true interest. I get it. After Tom died, I couldn't waste time on small talk. Not after the brevity of life had been so cruelly underscored.

"Ah, that's the Stonebridge tongue waggers is all. The gossip mill is great at embellishing the facts. I've been a lot of places, yes, but not even half of the world's nations."

She quickly opens the gift, and exclaims with delight at the lantern. Placing it back in the box, she sniffs, wipes her nose with a tissue she's taken out of an invisible side pocket.

"Your taste is exquisite, Angel. It's why I adore your shop." She takes a seat on a chaise and motions for me to take the one next to it, both under an umbrella, thank goodness. "Please, stay for a bit. Tell me what's going on in town. I've isolated myself up here since…" She doesn't have to say any more.

"I understand. So you're not back to work yet?"

"No, I had my receptionist reschedule everyone for two weeks out. That will be too soon, too, but I know myself well enough to realize I'm going to have to get back to my routine." She waves her arms about. "As you can see, it's easy for me to hide out here."

"It's only natural to want to be somewhere where you can lick your wounds. You need a safe place to process, Verity."

"Yes."

"Do you have family or friends who are supporting you?"

"My parents were here, but I made them go home. Mom comes in every morning so far, bringing me breakfast. She leaves my other meals, too. She's always spoiled me."

Phew. So she wasn't sitting here totally alone all day. That's a recipe for the kind of grief that turns into endless, and sometimes deadly, depression.

"You need all the TLC you can get right now. And it helps your loved ones, too."

"How do you mean?"

"No one knows what to do when you lose your husband

too soon. And Hank's death wasn't at all expected—"

"No, it sure wasn't." I think I hear a tremor of anger in her tone.

"I'm sorry." Her budding frustration is all part of the grieving process. She's going to get really upset with herself, at Hank for leaving, at everyone who comes near her. I know I did.

"It's so odd, isn't it? I mean, you must have gone through this. One minute I'm fine, almost in a surreal denial that it's happened, and the next, I'm hit by such…unimaginable…pain." She buries her face in her hands, sobs breaking through.

"Woof." Moose lays his large body over her legs and licks at her hands, trying to see her eyes.

My heart squeezes so tightly I can't draw a breath. I'm transported back to the initial grief I suffered at Tom's passing. It didn't matter that we'd had months to process the inevitable, that his final breath released him from the suffering his cancer brought. When Tom's soul left planet Earth, so did a piece of my heart.

"It's very hard, Verity. The worst." I spy a box of tissues on the table and grab several. "Here."

"Thanks." Tears drip from her jaw, and I'm done wrestling with my conscience. I remain standing, ready to leave. This can't be worth figuring out the murder right now, can it?

"It's so weird how I just knew he was gone, you know?"

Her words are sobering.

The patio chaise cushion embraces my bottom as I sit right back down.

"Oh? How do you mean?"

She pushes Moose off the chaise. "Lie down, that's a good boy." He complies and places his head on his paws, his gaze never leaving Verity.

"I'd been by your store earlier, as I'm sure you remember." She stops, stares at me. "You're the last person who saw us together as a couple."

"I am?" I already know this is a possibility from the ragged timeline I've pieced together, but having her confirmation helps me. Unless she's lying.

"Yes, and we weren't on our best behavior, were we? I don't know if you noticed, but we were squabbling. Two strong-willed people can do that." She offers a tremulous smile.

"I remember you were checking on your Japanese lantern."

"Yes." She nods. "Hank was eager to get on with our day—we cherish Saturday afternoons and all day Sunday off. We drove home and had lunch. I wanted to spend the day by the pool, maybe do a little gardening, but Hank asked me to wait until he got back. He made me promise to never swim on my own, for safety's sake. And he doesn't like me working in the yard without him around, just in case I hurt myself." She smiles as if his concern was sweet, but all I'm thinking is *control freak*.

"Back from where? He was going somewhere?"

"He took Moose for a walk. Usually they go in the mornings, when it's cooler, but we'd had other things on our mind that morning." That same smile comes back. "It was our anniversary. Ten years of a beautiful marriage. We'd recently decided it was time to start our family. We spent time in bed before we ran our errands."

"Before you stopped into my store?" My memory flashes to how dressed up Verity was.

"Ah, yes." Does Verity realize how cagey her tone is? "We were out here, actually, to celebrate. I know it's probably odd to you, being from such a regimented background and all, but let me just say that Hank and I valued our privacy. That morning, we were celebrating all the previous times we've made love right here, on the banks of Jacob's Run."

My mind conjures up how Ava and Lily would react to Verity's declaration. Fortunately, I keep my lips sealed on this one and don't burst out with "ick," or "TMI." And in truth, it's possible that both girls would find Verity's admission romantic.

If I'm going to help Trinity with this case, I can't afford to take either view. *Just the facts, ma'am.*

"You said Hank took Moose for a walk?" I prompt.

"Yes. All you have to do is cut through our yard, over there"—Verity points at a spot in the center of a copse of trees—"and within five minutes, you're on the actual Jacob's Run path. It comes out where the public launches their kayaks and god-awful floats from. You wouldn't believe what people consider legit water transport around here." She laughs. I smile and nod along, but inside I'm sad at her disrespect of Uma. Verity's snobby observation about the rest of us mortals who don't have our own private launch area is disappointing. I want to relate to her as a sister widow, but we are on different frequencies on other things.

"So he went for walk..." I prompt again.

"Yes. And I never saw him again." Verity sighs, followed by a long pause. Sweet cardinal song is oblivious to the sorrow that shrouds our conversation. The rapid dart of a hummingbird among a spill of honeysuckle against the pool fence seems to reiterate the concept of life being too short, no matter when it ends.

"It was about an hour later that Moose found me. I was pruning the rose arbor, thinking about what we'd do for dinner. We're not big on going out, even for our tenth. That dog scared the devil out of me, pushing his wet nose against my leg. He was soaked. Now that I know Hank was shot, I realize how much it must have frightened Moose. Isn't that right, big boy?" She rubs the dog's ears and leans closer to him so that his tongue can reach his chin. "He'd escaped his leash, and leather collar, but still had his flea and tick collar on; it's a miracle it didn't get caught on anything."

"Were you worried that Hank wasn't with him?" I know

that I'm leading her, but I'm not the DA and this isn't an interrogation.

"Worried?" She seems genuinely perplexed. "Oh, you mean because Moose came back alone, without Hank?"

I nod.

"Not at all. Not right away. Hank lets Moose come home on his own a lot. But he usually unclips the leash first. That was my first red flag, when I saw his leather collar was gone."

I have to ask Nate about this, since he's the one with a dog. I know what Ralph does whenever I get hurt. He screeches at the top of his birdie lungs, mimicking me perfectly. "*Help, help*" and "*ouch*" are in his repertoire. He does it every time I stub my toe, and on the occasions that he's bitten me hard enough to break my skin.

It makes no sense to me that Moose would have left Hank alone to die. Unless he's afraid of loud noises, like a gunshot.

Or if he knew someone he trusted was in the area. But Trinity all but said it was a shot by an experienced shooter. I look at Verity with the eyes of an investigator. Sure, she's a chiropractor, a healer by trade. But that doesn't mean she doesn't know her way around a rifle. And someone who knows the intricacies of the human skeleton would be able to clean up any and all evidence including gunpowder and the murder weapon, right?

Chapter Thirteen

I CALL TRINITY on my drive back from Verity's, as per our agreement. I run down everything I think I unearthed. And end with my question.

"Why would a dog leave its injured—or dead—owner like that?"

"Who knows? It's probably what Verity already told you. A lot of dogs are afraid of any kind of loud, sudden noise like a gunshot. Verity Price's alibi checks out, Angel. She was home alone at the time of Hank's murder, and we have proof of it on the house's video security feed. There's no weapon, no sign of them having other guns. We have to spread our net wider." Trinity's voice fills my car through the hands-free phone.

"She did seem genuinely bereaved, for the most part," I admit. "But then again, she'd act as if nothing happened, too."

"No two people process a murder the same way, Angel."

"I know that."

"Something else is bothering you about your talk with Verity. I can hear it in your voice. What is it?"

"I don't like that she doesn't come right out and say that Hank wasn't practicing, that he was solely a business manager. I feel as though there's more, that she's holding something back. I don't know what it is. And while the evidence doesn't support that she's the murderer, she could have become angry enough with Hank to do it. She described the argument I witnessed as a simple squabble. I'm telling you, it was more than that. As for the trying to get pregnant part, that seemed a little contrived to me."

"Do you have proof they weren't doing that? Trying for a baby?" she asks.

"Of course not!"

Trinity laughs. "Thanks for keeping me informed. I'll see you in the morning for coffee, okay?"

"Sure thing."

We end the call and I don't stop thinking about Moose or Verity the entire drive back to town.

I'M MEETING CRYSTAL at Latte Love, but I show up twenty minutes early so that I can talk to Nate first. My fingers are crossed that he'll be available. He's not at the counter, so I ask the barista, who is tying his apron, clearly coming in to start his shift. I don't recognize him but his name tag says KEVIN MOORE.

"Yes, he's in, but let me see if he's available. Please wait here." Kevin doesn't know me yet, and it'd be awkward to blurt out that I'm Nate's gal pal. The other baristas would send me right back. I don't push it as I don't want to seem presumptuous and I'm not certain how much Nate wants a new employee to know about his personal life. I texted him before I came over, and he said he was in.

Kevin disappears for a brief moment to Nate's office, and returns, giving me a quick wave. "Go on in."

Nate stands when I walk in, which makes my tummy all warm inside. Mach trots up to greet me, too, and I bend down to pet him. I don't have to reach very far as Mach's head comes to my waist. When I'm done with Mach, I look up at Nate.

"Hey."

"Hey yourself. Come here." He opens his arms and I comply—why wouldn't I?—by taking the few steps to him. We share a brief kiss and a lovely hug. Mach grows bored with our PDA and lies down in the corner.

"I wish it was the weekend already." I break away and plop into the worn easy chair across from his desk. His laptop is open and pushed to the side, piles of papers that I assume are bills in the center. "Are those all bills? Aren't you paperless?"

He scratches the sides of his jaw. "I am, but a couple of my vendors still insist on paper trails. I've been here almost two years, and I'm still tracking down billers that the previous owner used."

"That's something I didn't have to deal with."

"Starting from scratch has its challenges, too," Nate says. He reminds me with a simple statement that he's one of the most generous people I've ever known.

"It does, but look how much you've changed, even in the time I've been back. You've completely remodeled, from paint to floors to lighting."

"The place needed an infusion of modern practicality." He studies me. "As much as I cherish our time together, you didn't stop by during a busy workday to compliment me. Am I right?"

A girl could get lost in his stormy gray eyes.

"You know me well. No, I'm not here to chitchat. I'm doing research of a sort."

"Research meaning you're digging in deeper to Hank Price's murder."

"Yes."

"Okay, shoot." We both wince. "Not the best choice of words, sorry," Nate says.

"It's about dogs."

As if he knows we're discussing his species, Mach sits up from his bed—aka a twin-size mattress—in the far corner of Nate's office.

"I'm sorry I'm interrupting your nap break, Mach." He yawns in response and lies back down with a protracted groan. "I'm getting used to his verbalizations, but he still sounds like he's in so much pain."

"It's a Shiloh shepherd trait, for sure, but Mach's personality plays a big part in his shenanigans."

"Great, so that already helps with my question. I'm trying to figure out what an average dog would do if they were walking with their owner, and something happened to their owner. Would the dog run off, or stay nearby, try to help them?"

"You mean if I got shot like Hank did, while I was walking Mach?"

"Yes."

"Sounds like you've been investigating," he observes.

Under Nate's knowing stare, I sag back in my chair. "Oh, okay. So I stopped by Verity's on the way over here. Hey, I told you last night that Trinity gave me the go-ahead."

Nate laughs, that deep belly kind that makes my skin tingle in anticipation of…you know. I've always professed that while a handsome guy is a great thing, the man who makes me laugh aloud will be able to get my clothes off. For all the right reasons, of course.

"You sure you're a combat veteran? Because I can read you so well, Angel. You don't keep anything hidden in your expressions."

"It's only because it's you, Nate."

"Stop with the ego stroking. I'll answer your question." He leans forward, and his strong arms settle atop the papers. "I'd like to think Mach would never leave my side. Or, if I needed help that he couldn't give me, that he'd go off and alert someone. But the reality?" He leans back in his chair far enough to reach Mach. His strong hand engulfs mine, yet next to the shepherd's humongous head, Nate's fingers look like a child's as he scratches Mach behind the ears. Mach sighs, but it resembles a moan of pleasure more than the grousing he does as he lies down.

"What do you think, Mach?" Nate muses.

I wait, not wanting to sway his response. Part of being a decent amateur detective is knowing when to keep my mouth *chiuso*, as in closed. It was one of the first Italian words my family learned when we were stationed in Naples, along with the twins' favorite dish, *pizza Margherita con prosciutto*.

"Nope," Nate says as he sits back up. "No way would Mach stay with me, not if a gunshot is involved. You've seen how much he loves fireworks."

I was at Nate's one night when his neighbors set off fireworks. At the first pop, Mach tried to curl his over one-hundred-pound mass of doggie love into Nate's lap. It was heart-wrenching to see how upset he was.

"Oh, you're right. There was no way to console him."

"No. If the Prices' dog is anything like Mach, then yeah, a gunshot could have been enough to send him home. Except..."

"What?"

Nate shakes his head. "A thunderstorm or fireworks

makes sense because they last for longer than one second. A gunshot is one and done. That would startle Mach, and he'd do a bit of a freak out, but I'd like to think he'd come back to me right after."

I think back to how Bryce and I heard the firework. As sure as I am that's what it was, I have to face the fact that Bryce and I were wrong. We heard a gunshot. Unless the killer used a silencer. But there had been a gunshot as evidenced by Hank's murder. Could there have been two sounds? A dog's acute hearing would detect both, no problem. I don't know what the police have found out from the other people in the area, though. It's another question for Trinity.

"Thanks for listening to me and answering my dog question."

"I'd like to think you stopped by for more than that." Nate grins.

"Actually, I'm meeting Crystal but I came early, hoping you'd be in."

"What time are you meeting your sister?"

I glance at my phone. "In ten minutes."

"Then what are you waiting for? Come here." He winks.

Far be it from me to turn down a request from the silver fox barista.

Chapter Fourteen

ELEVEN MINUTES LATER, I'm sitting out front with Crystal, thinking about how Latte Love has a whole new meaning for me since meeting Nate. We're in our favorite spot, in the back corner booth that affords us a perfect view of the entire shop while giving us a modicum of privacy.

The coffee shop is bustling for a midweek late morning. Our table's vantage, kitty-corner from the espresso bar, allows me to watch Nate without being too stalker about it. He's in his element, pulling steaming shots while charming the customers. Nate wouldn't hear of using the espresso brewers that are totally automatic and require a mere press of a button. Save that for the chain coffee shops.

I have to admit that there's a real skill, a talent, to making a perfect espresso drink. And I'm not the only one who's noticing Nate's skill level.

Two women take their time ordering drinks and baked goods, quizzing Nate about the intricacies of each ad infinitum. I would think that unless you have a health concern like celiac disease, there are only so many questions one can ask about the ingredients in Latte Love's banana bread, which is definitely not gluten free. Yet the woman with a platinum bob giggles after she asks about nutmeg, and the woman she's with beams at Nate as though he's giving them a secret recipe. It's not unlike the scene at a bar during happy hour. Except the customers in this shop seem to be happy no matter the time of day.

It's all about Nate. He credits Amy, the woman who now works in my shop, too, for the decor and overall welcoming ambiance. But he's the brains behind creating a local coffee shop that's as welcoming to Stonebridge natives as the scores of day-trippers who descend from their tour buses.

"It's nice to see you focused on something besides a murder," Crystal says.

"Mmm?" I'm still watching Nate.

Nate offers an affable grin to the fawning customers, talking up the talents of his baker as he froths milk with practiced ease. He pours the milk into two tall glasses and quickly rounds the counter, heading straight for our table. We make eye contact, and my stomach does that free fall I'm still not used to.

"One latte for my sweetheart and one for her sister." He sets the drinks in front of us.

"Thanks, Nate." Crystal pours a liberal dose of turbinado sugar into her glass.

"Yes, thank you, Nate." The other customers' stares would be hilarious if I didn't know I'm as red as the petunias blooming from the cup and saucer planter on the counter. I don't let my discomfort stop me from giving him a smile, from looking into his eyes. He rewards me with today's second wink. I swear I hear the women at the table nearest our booth sigh.

"Always."

He turns and walks back behind the espresso bar. Starting a fresh shot, he describes his movements to the man standing next to him. He's training the new barista, Kevin. Nate mentioned he'd recently hired someone who had retired but desired to be more a part of the community. It's a reflection of what I love about my hometown. We don't conform to expectations of a sleepy small town. A good thing when examining inclusive hiring practices, not so great when tabulating our recent homicide statistics.

"Earth to Angel." Crystal taps on the table. "Although I totally understand your distraction."

"Sorry. I was wondering how it's going for Nate with the new guy." Yeah, I'm not telling Crystal about the more intimate aspects of my relationship with Nate. Those talks are for Trinity, if anyone. My sister and I agreed to meet early today, instead of our usual time of midmorning on the weekend. It's three days since I found Hank's body, and as Crystal put it, "about time you let me know what you're cooking up."

"Poor Kevin. I'm glad he's found something to do." Crystal sighs and takes a sip of her pistachio latte. I'm slowly sipping my lavender cardamom latte. I don't want to ruin the latte art Nate made me. The froth depicts a woman with shoulder-length hair, sitting in lotus position. With a large bird on her shoulder.

"Why poor him? What's going on?"

"His wife just died, after he took care of her for years. She was disabled."

"That is sad. I'm sorry to hear it." And once again my experience with losing Tom comes into play. I didn't caretake for Tom as long as Kevin did his wife, but the several months were long enough. It's more than a glimpse of hell to watch your beloved fail and then die. My sore heart reminds me that I need to be careful to not internalize every widowed spouse's pain. Verity's suffering definitely affected me more than I anticipated, and it's still lingering. "I wonder why he decided to work here?"

"Kevin told Brad that he doesn't have to work, but had to get out of the house, start to socialize with people again. We used to see him and Mabel all about town. She was the local head librarian for years."

"I don't know Kevin or Mabel. What is his last name?"

"Moore. Mabel Moore started working at the library while you were in the navy, up until she absolutely couldn't anymore, about six months ago. And she was in a chair. Not paralyzed but her back gave her enough trouble that it was easier for her to get around in the chair. She usually sat at the circulation desk."

"But she could walk?"

"Yes. I never saw her without a walker or two crutches, though. You know, the kind you lean on with your forearms."

"Was she disabled her whole life?"

"No clue."

"What did she die of?"

"Whoa, Sherlock Warren. You're still in investigator mode, I can see."

"Sorry." There won't be any stopping me until I have all the answers I need for Hank Price's murder. It's no excuse for me to be so nosy about a stranger-to-me, though.

"Ultimately I think it was her heart that gave out. Such a shame, after all she did to stay active. I'd see her at the Y, doing pool laps the same time as me. Kevin would wait in the car, at that ungodly hour." Crystal likes to get her workouts done before seven a.m. We're a family of early risers.

"I remember the feeling that Kevin's having now. Needing to have something to do that has nothing to do with what you've just been through. A distraction. I could have opted to not work for at least a few years after I retired from the navy, if the girls didn't have college."

"So why didn't you?"

"Tom and I saved for the twins' education, and we had some extra military benefits that have helped a lot. Yet we could never have afforded to send them both away at the same time."

"So you started the shop."

"Yes. For the money, of course. But it was more than that, Sis. The thought of an empty house, without Tom or the girls around…" I sigh and take a healthy swig of my coffee. *What was I saying about distractions?* "This is delicious."

"And you're surprised?" Crystal asks.

"No."

"What is it?" Crystal's being a parrot with a nut again.

"I'm thinking my latte's tastier than yours because there's an extra ingredient in mine. Nate added his undying adoration of me."

"That is sickeningly sweet," Crystal says.

"You asked." I know I'm smirking.

"So tell me the details, Sister." Crystal raises her brows, pressing her lips into a thin line. I squirm despite the fact we're no longer kids; Crystal isn't telling me what to do while our parents are out. I have to come clean with her on what I'm doing as far as the investigation is concerned. She won't tolerate a noncommittal reply. We have the blessing of a sister relationship that allows us to butt heads quite often without ruining our strong bond. We're not as intuitive with one another as my girls are; we're not twins. But we are from the same mold.

"There isn't a whole lot of information yet, Crystal."

"Spare me, spare you. Spare both of us the runaround.

Tell. Me. Now."

I sit up taller, square my shoulders, lean in. "Okay. There's not a whole lot that I know about Hank and Verity, except that Verity has really good taste in decor and is one of my most dependable customers." I detail my trip to visit Verity, my impressions so far. "Did you know that Hank didn't see patients? Ever?"

"What?" Crystal's agape.

"Apparently, he ran the business side of things to free up Verity to do all of the actual chiropractic work."

"That is odd. I mean, not that it's unheard of for business partners to divvy up responsibilities like that. Except, Hank is, um, was a chiropractor, too, right? All the ads I've ever seen show photos of them as a couple, right?" Her brows draw together.

"You are correct. I know, I wondered at first if I'd been obtuse to miss that. They do give the impression of both seeing patients, don't they?"

"I'll say." Crystal taps on her phone. She holds it up for my viewing. "Look at this. It doesn't say anywhere that it's not both of them treating."

"I get the part about having someone else do the numbers. I'd love to have someone else handling my books. Heck, I'm thrilled I found Amy to take over the website and social media, plus work some retail hours."

"You got lucky with her, no question." Crystal nods toward Nate, who is pouring steamed froth into a to-go cup,

Kevin intently observing. "Doesn't Nate miss having Amy around?"

"I don't think so. She's still on his payroll, does his social, and she handles Latte Love's seasonal decor." Which is why I was drawn to Amy in the first place. Her appreciation of aesthetics. Latte Love is decked out for July, from the paper red, white, and blue bunting that hangs from the espresso bar, to the foil faux sparklers that perch in clear blue Mason jars on each café table. The red petunias I described earlier are the cherry on the festive trimmings.

"She's a talent," Crystal says.

"Unlike me, Nate enjoys doing his own accounting, and like me, he doesn't trust ordering to anyone else. He'll let his two assistant managers order regular goods like paper mugs and drink stirrers. But he's the only one who picks out the beans."

"Which makes this shop one of a kind. I notice that she's adopted some of your taste." She points to the dazzling coffee counter. "Not as over-the-top, more streamlined."

I laugh. "Since when have you ever used *streamlined* to describe me?"

We both chuckle. Growing up, Crystal and I shared a room and my side was without question the messiest.

"You always could find whatever you were looking for, I'll give you that."

"Well, I've taken a page out of your organizational skills book. You'll be happy to know that as of last month my inventory is completely digitized. Everything that's on a shelf or in the storage room matches the corresponding spreadsheet."

"I'm so glad you did that. I'd be lost without my spreadsheets. Between the live flower shipments and wide range of decorative merchandise, not to mention vases, I'd be lost." Crystal bites into a blueberry and strawberry scone, the white icing a perfect foil for the red and blue flag-shaped sprinkles. "Oh my goodness, I should have bought three of these."

I laugh, pointing to my large, empty ramekin. "That's why I always get the baked oatmeal. If I start on pastries for breakfast, I'm into the sweets all day."

"That's ridiculous. You know better than to eat too much."

"Hmm." Crystal's so sure of her opinion that I don't have the heart to tell her that she's wrong. Some of us can't stop at one sugary treat, and I happen to be one of them. I thank my navy training and knowing how icky I'll feel if I indulge in sweets for why I don't give in to the constant temptation. Stonebridge has no shortage of ways to feed a sweet tooth, with its own bakery, an ice cream shop, and a Belgian chocolatier.

"You're right. I don't need more than one of these."

"But you'll take some home for 'Brad,' right?" We laugh.

"There is something I didn't mention Sunday night at your place."

"Go on."

"I don't like how Hank treated Verity. I wasn't friends with either of them, not at all. Like I said, she's little more than an acquaintance, truth be told. A valued customer whom I always felt I could be comfortable around." Until the lantern fiasco. "I recently have had to tell Verity that something she ordered right after Christmas still isn't in. She wasn't happy, which is understandable. I took accountability, but I was getting her to understanding that it wasn't the shop's fault, that it was the supply chain causing the delay. But Hank"—I shake my head—"Hank was a different story." I quickly summarize how Hank behaved last Saturday, from his curious inspection of my wares to his arrogance over the late order. "He would have humiliated me if he could have, but I'm way beyond that by now."

"Don't mess with a navy pilot!" Crystal can never hold back her pride over my military service. It's sweet and touching, if a little over-the-top. I flew helicopters, not fighter jets.

"Something like that. I don't give a flip how he spoke to me, but the shade he was throwing Verity was beyond my tolerance level. Not that it matters at this point. Now that I've found out she might be in money trouble, I understand their bickering a little better. And I'm wondering if they weren't the successful entrepreneurs everyone thinks they are."

"According to this real estate app, their house alone is worth over a million." Crystal's addicted to all home-buying apps. "Not that how much their property's worth doesn't matter as much as their cashflow. If Verity could afford expensive knickknacks, I'd say they were doing all right."

"But she always paid with a credit card," I counter.

"Really? But doesn't everyone these days?"

I nod. "No one carries around large amounts of cash these days."

"There's a way in, Angel, and I have confidence you'll figure it out."

"I have to admit I felt a bit like a creep, snooping around Verity earlier. If she's guilty of anything, she's one good actor."

"It's not snooping if it helps Trinity catch the killer faster."

"That's my story!" I grin.

"Did you get any scary vibes when you were with her?"

"Now you sound like Eloise."

"Hey, we're given an instinct for a reason."

"We are." I think for a minute. "I have a hard time believing she has a nefarious bone in her body, when she spends all day adjusting bones so that people feel better. Yet after I saw how Hank talked to her, I'd understand the anger, rage even, at being talked down to like that. But for it to lead to murder? And it would mean she knows how to fire a weapon."

"That's not unusual around these parts. Lots of women shoot these days. There's the Stonebridge Hunting Sisterhood, for example."

"I know. And the gauge of the bullet is definitely one a deer hunter uses. But it was fired from a good distance away, up to four hundred yards according to Trinity. That makes a circle that crosses to the other side of Jacob's Run."

"Yeah, but the direction the bullet was fired from?"

"If it didn't ricochet, Trinity thinks it could have come from anywhere within range, frankly. The new subdivisions, the older ones…" I go on and mention the literally dozens of places a shooter could have aimed from.

"They'd have to know Hank was going to be there, though."

"Yes. Or waited for him." I think about how Verity mentioned it wasn't the usual time Hank walked Moose. Would a killer wait hours to take out their victim, when it's such a busy time of year on Jacob's Run?

Crystal fiddles with her napkin. "I'm worried about you, Angel. You've been back for only a year but it feels like you've never left. It would kill me if anything ever happened to you, Sis. No pun intended."

I blink. Several times. Then I lean over and give Crystal a big hug. "Nothing's going to happen to me. I've got you." I pull back after Crystal lets her stiff defense down enough to hug me back. "Plus Trinity's a true friend. She gets me and my need to figure things out when I can, but she isn't afraid to put me in my place. I'm definitely an all-volunteer investigator of the facts." I wait for Crystal to laugh but she's not having it.

"You'll always be my little sis, Angel."

"Thanks."

My phone rings and at one glance the intimate moment evaporates. "It's Mom."

Crystal looks at her watch, then bites her lower lip. "Hmm. That's odd. Isn't she supposed to be in State College this week?" Our mother spearheads the Stonebridge Historical Society's archaeological committee, which is in fact what we refer to in our family as the eel weir campaign. She spends a lot of time lobbying Penn State's Anthropology Department—which oversees all things archaeological—wooing them to do a dig right here, in Jacob's Run. Since the university seat is in State College, two hours away, she often stays overnight when she's visiting on one of her "research" trips.

I keep my phone on the table, put it on speaker.

"Hi, Mom. I'm here with Crystal. We thought you were in State College."

"Thank goodness you answered!" Her breathless exclamation raises the hairs on my nape. Mom is the steady person in our family, more stoic than Crystal.

"Mom, what's wrong?"

"I don't want to worry the rest of the family, but I need you to pick me up from the hospital."

"In State College?"

"No, no, I came back last night. And I brought an assistant professor, you know, a researcher, with me. But when we were looking at the weir site, you know, in Jacob's Run, a funny thing happened." Her breathing is labored and I think I make out other voices, maybe some indistinguishable *beeps*. *Where is she?*

"Mom, it's Crystal. Where are you?"

She doesn't reply and there's a lot of rustling sounds, which only ratchets up my anxiety. Crystal's gaping stare isn't helping. We're poised over my phone, as if willing her to tell us she's okay, it's not as bad as it sounds.

"Mom?" I'm struggling to keep a neutral face while my insides do the mambo.

"Angel, it's Trinity. Your mother's going to be fine, but sore for a while. She has a graze across her front side."

"A graze?"

"Yes."

"As in a bullet graze?" I ignore Crystal's gasp but wince when she puts a clawlike grasp on my forearm.

"Affirmative. I'll wait here until you arrive. And Angel?" Trinity's voice goes from soothing to detective mode with her query.

"Yes?"

"Don't discuss this with anyone else."

"Uh...okay."

"Who's with you?"

"Crystal's sitting here with me. We're at the coffee shop."

"Tell me I'm not on speaker phone."

"You're not on speaker phone?" Crystal asks.

Trinity's sigh sounds more like a *thump* against the mic. "Fine. See you both soon. But don't rush, take your time. It's not life-threatening."

It's life-altering, though. For all of us.

Chapter Fifteen

I T TAKES CRYSTAL and me ten minutes flat to get to the hospital ER, where we're taken back to the treatment area as soon as we identify ourselves. Trinity must have told the front desk to expect us. The advantage of living in such a tight-knit community isn't lost on me. When I was stationed in a metropolitan area or overseas, where our family knew few if any persons not in the military, civilian hospitals could feel more like fortresses than places of healing.

"Let me make sure it's okay with the attending to have both of you go in together." The nurse motions for us to wait outside the small room. The curtains are drawn over the windows so there's nothing to see.

"Are we sure Trinity said it wasn't life-threatening?" Crystal whispers.

"Positive." I nod as if I'm certain Mom's okay, but my noodle knees betray my facade of confidence.

"It can't be that bad if she's out here. When Brad sliced his finger off last summer with a hedge trimmer, they took him right into surgery." I know Crystal's doing her version of the cup is half full but the warrior in me is riled. Our mother's been shot. At the same place Hank was shot *dead*.

"They saved Brad's finger." My words come out on a whisper and I feel, rather than see, Crystal's hand grab my elbow and shove me into a nearby chair. I've closed my eyes, my go-to when I need to go inward, away from something I don't want to deal with.

"Don't lose it now, Sister. I need you!" Her ferocious demand is what I need. My eyes snap open.

"Right." I want to tell her that the only reason I could possibly get faint is because I know she's here. It's not like I'm flying a mission and the entire crew is depending on me to land the helicopter safely. But all I can do is stare at my sister, nod my head.

"You okay?" she asks.

"Yes." I nod. "Yes, I'm okay. Really." The events of the past several days have caught up with me is all. The further I am from my military life and needing to be stalwart, the more my emotions can surface without warning.

The nurse pokes her head around the entry. "Okay, you come on in, but please stay out of the doctor's way."

Mom's sitting back on a bed. Trinity's standing in a corner, arms crossed as she watches the scene. We exchange a quick glance, the kind I've shared with countless fellow officers or sailors over the years. It's a grave situation, but an expert is taking care of it. For now.

Mom's eyes look like they do when she hears of a sudden death in the family as the doctor speaks to her in low, soothing tones. My guess is she's still in shock, from what I'm witnessing and my limited combat experience. The doctor appears to be finishing up with a bandage on Mom's lower front right rib cage. I take a deep breath in, exhale. This isn't a war zone, it's Stonebridge. The modern hospital with all of its high tech tells me I'm in a safe place, and I try to cling to this thought. Seeing my mother after she's been shot is less than reassuring, however.

The doctor peels off her latex gloves, throws them in the trash, and washes her hands at the sink. No longer blocked by the physician, Mom's gaze wanders. When she sees Crystal and me, her eyes fill.

"My girls!" She leans forward, winces. "Come here, give me a kiss. No hugs, though, please."

"Mom." We take turns giving her a kiss on the cheek.

"Doctor, you can say anything you need to in front of these three. They're my daughters. Trinity's my adopted daughter." Mom tears up again. Crystal and I are each holding one of her hands. Trinity takes two steps to reach our circle and places her hand on Mom's shoulder.

"Nice to meet you." I start to raise my free hand to shake the doctor's hand before remembering she probably doesn't want my germs.

Dr. Archana Sengupta—I read her name tag—smiles and gives me and Crystal each a nod. "Your mother is quite the superhero today. You can be very proud of her."

"Enough of that, Archana." Mom's already made best

friends with the woman, which is no surprise. We joke all the time that she needs to run for mayor. "What's the holdup? Can I leave now?"

"Hold on. You've escaped with a *graze*, but don't mistake such a benign term for a minor injury. You didn't get directly hit, the injury is only superficial, but the abrasion needs to be watched. I'd like a medical professional to change your bandage the first time, and then see how you feel about doing it yourself thereafter."

"But—" Mom is probably seeing this as an inconvenience to her full schedule.

Dr. Sengupta holds up her hands. "Hang on. The wound care is the physical part. The other side of this coin is that you've been shot. The bullet didn't cause major physical damage, but the mental and emotional components can be difficult to navigate. That's why we asked whether or not you have support at home."

"I do. My one daughter"—Mom points to me—"is a retired navy pilot. She's been in combat. You can handle washing a wound out, can't you, honey? My other daughter"—she nods at Crystal—"is an excellent caretaker. She kept me and my husband hydrated through an awful bought of food poisoning earlier this year. And Trinity's a detective, the tops in Harrisburg before she transferred to Stonebridge." Mom's blathering makes me inwardly wince. How must Crystal feel when Mom points to me first? Crystal's always been here for our parents while I've been globe-trotting.

"Crystal knows your entire medical history, Mom," I say. "My first aid training doesn't qualify me to do a whole lot. We'll make sure you get in with your GP. How soon, Doctor?"

"Tomorrow morning without exception. We'll give you a care sheet with your discharge papers. Take the ibuprofen and acetaminophen as directed to stay ahead of the discomfort." It's clear that Dr. Sengupta is reiterating her instructions for all of us, as Mom's most likely not going to remember a lot of this.

"I feel fine. It's just a little numb," Mom says.

"That's because we administered a local anesthetic for the initial cleaning. It's going to bother you for at least the next few days. Don't get it wet tonight, either, okay?" Dr. Sengupta looks at Mom, her gaze gentle.

"Yes," Crystal and I reply in unison. Usually we giggle after we do this, say the same thing at the same time without planning it.

There's no giggling now, though.

Dr. Sengupta leaves and the nurse comes in to go over the discharge paperwork. Crystal taps me on the shoulder.

"You go outside with Trinity and find out what really happened," she whispers. "I'll get Mom home."

"I'll be right behind you," I say.

"Sounds good. And go ahead and call Bryce, will you?" she asks.

"Got it. What about Dad?" I ask.

"I'll tell him," Crystal says, then looks at her phone. "He should be finishing up his second round about now. He'll probably get home right as we do." Dad's an obsessive golfer and rarely misses a summer morning out on the course.

"Okay. Call me if you need me sooner. Thanks, Crystal." We hug and I blink back tears for the second time today. I'm not one for sunshine platitudes in the midst of ugly events, but I can't deny the warmth that Crystal's trust wraps around my heart. It feels wonderful to be part of the family team, up close and personal.

TRINITY AND I walk out together, not stopping until we reach the parking lot. We stand under a Japanese maple tree, the late-afternoon breeze rustling the leaves above us.

"Thank you so much for taking care of my mom."

"Hey, like she said, she's as much my mom as yours." Trinity looks over the dozens of parked cars with the same professional eye I've watched her employ at crime scenes. It takes me a minute to realize she's not looking for criminals but rather, words. "She got lucky, Angel."

Her declaration strikes cold fear through my chest.

"What is going on in our town, Trinity?"

"That's what I'm working to find out," she says.

"I know I'm not a pro like you, but can you give me your

impression of what happened? I need your take before my mom tells me her version. You know Livvie Strooper, she'll turn a trip to the grocery store into the secrets of a lost civilization." My mother's full name is Olivia, but my dad, Douglas Strooper, has always called her Livvie.

Trinity snorts. "That's the truth. The short version is that she was in the water, at Jacob's Run, with a researcher from Penn State. She was showing him the weir, and he was using an underwater camera. Does that make sense to you?"

"Yes. You already know Mom's obsessed with proving the weir is as old as the pyramids of Egypt. She needs the experts to do it, though, so she's been going to State College to talk to the Anthropology Department in person. Think of her as the Jacob's Run weir lobbyist." I stare at Trinity. "Wait a minute. Where is the researcher who was with her?"

"We're on it. A call came in reporting the incident. Your mother claims that this man"—Trinity glanced at her tablet—"Fred Unser, walked her over to the bank and sat her down right after it happened, and used his phone to call 9-1-1. But then he walked away. When I arrived on scene, there was no sign he'd ever been there."

"What about his phone number?"

"Burner. Fortunately for us, he called the station about twenty minutes after his first call. He says he was scared and drove to a Sheetz, which is where my officer met up with him." She refers to a popular gas station.

"He left my mother alone, after she'd been shot at." My

hands tighten into balls as I imagine taking the "researcher" down with my bare hands.

"He called it in, though. Fred Unser had a burner because he says he lost his regular phone and didn't want to tell his parents. Grad students are often still on the family dole," Trinity says.

"My mother's not stupid, Trinity. You know that. She wouldn't meet up with someone she hasn't met. But she let him go with her, even though they'd never met?" I grasp for a lead.

"I hear you. It turns out this particular researcher showed up instead of the professor who'd promised to be here. Your mother had no reason to doubt the man who did show; he said he was a TA working toward his PhD. We've verified that he works at Penn State, and we're checking that he doesn't have any priors. The last part is routine for us. I don't have any reason to think an anthropology TA would have criminal intent except that this one disappeared right after Livvie was shot."

"What about a bullet at the scene?" I ask.

"My officers are still there, collecting evidence, but finding the bullet like we did at Hank's murder scene isn't a given."

"But her wound, that has to tell us something?" I ask.

"It's almost impossible to tell what kind of bullet made a graze wound," she says.

"What are you thinking, Trin? Why would anyone shoot

my mother?" My voice involuntarily increases in pitch.

"I'm not thinking anything right now. We don't have enough information. I've got an officer on the way to State College, two others making calls. We'll have more answers by morning. We still have an unknown and unidentified shooter for Hank Price, and now a second for your mom. It could be someone who doesn't like people doing anything near the weir, or two separate shooters. I need you to convince your mother to stay out of Jacob's Run and away from that site until we have all the answers."

The weir had been an issue in our high school classmate's murder last year, too. Most of the town was ambivalent about whether it will turn into its own tourist destination. There are two smaller factions, though. One that is doing everything they can to figure out the weir's origins, aka my mom. Mom spearheaded the formation of the committee pushing to determine the weir's age. A handful of members joined, and now there are a couple dozen members. The antiweir folks are composed of two seemingly disparate groups. One is staunch in not giving a hoot about history and only caring that their private properties aren't disturbed by researchers and resultant tourists. The other faction of the leave-it-alone group believes the weir, if ancient, is sacred and shouldn't be touched. Both groups of weir naysayers show up at town hall meetings, express their distress over digging up the past, and write letters to the editor.

But would any of them be so irate they'd kill to squelch

Mom's weir project?

"Hank Price was on the eel weir committee, too. Do you think that's what this is all about, the weir?"

"Again, I don't know, Angel. We have a lot of people with loud voices who want no part of an archaeological excavation in Stonebridge. And it goes beyond our town. If they shut down Jacob's Run to do the research, or if it turns out to be ancient and it's turned into a national historic site, it will affect the waterways surrounding Stonebridge, all the way to the Susquehanna."

"Which widens the pool of suspects, even if we're talking about only one or two extremists."

"Yes." She blows out a breath, hands on her hips.

"Has there been anything uncovered about Verity's finances? I'm wondering if everything Eloise told me has panned out as truth," I say.

"Yes, there seems to be a problem with their cashflow. I can confirm that her bank accounts are depleted."

"But you can't tell me the exact deets. I understand. So we're still looking at the possibility that Verity has a motive related to money?"

"Verity or whomever Hank was giving their money to, if we can prove he was the one who took the funds out. If Verity is playing us, she's very clever, I'll give her that. We'll get to the bottom of it all, Angel, but it's got to be sooner than later. I don't want one more person harmed."

"So you're closing the creek off?"

She nods. "Until further notice. We have to figure this out, Angel."

"We will."

I notice she says "we" and doesn't blink when I do, too. It's not the time to gloat over being brought in on the case, though.

Like I was ever out of it.

Chapter Sixteen

AFTER TRINITY'S WARNING, I dropped by Mom's. I had to see that she was doing fine. Crystal had everything under control, so I didn't stay long. Bryce showed up while I was there, still upset with Crystal and me that we hadn't called him immediately.

By the time I left my parents, all I wanted was a long soak in my claw-foot tub. I texted Nate to tell him that it might be easier to skip our dinner tonight, as I didn't know when I'd be home. He replied that he'd be by with a pizza "because the girls still need to eat, after all." Which is why we're sitting at the kitchen table, each of us in our own funk over Mom being shot.

"This is so not how I expected my first summer off in college to go." Ava helps herself to a slice of Hawaiian pizza. We pass around the large monkeypod bowl, using the modern necessity of lime-green silicone-tipped tongs to grab generous portions of a tossed green salad. Tomatoes are plentiful at the farmers' market and the mix of red, orange, and yellow varieties makes the simple salad as eye-pleasing as it is delicious. The girls share a pizza while Nate and I devour a sushi platter. Nate treated with takeout after he heard about Mom's adventure.

"No kidding. I'm so glad Grandma's okay!" Lily picks the ham off her slice.

"I would have ordered half with just pineapple, Lily." Nate's still tiptoeing a bit around the girls, as if nineteen-year-old women are an enigma. For the record, they are.

"Oh, this is fine, Nate, thank you. I like the smoky flavor of the ham, but I don't like the texture. It feels weird against my teeth."

"Oh. Okay. Good to know." Nate's quintessential masculine features redden, making his silver hair and whiskers more pronounced. He doesn't have a full beard, per se, but the right amount of growth on his chin and jawline to take his sexiness to the exact point that blows my skirt up. Sorry, it's a lewd expression I learned in the navy. But apropos for me and Nate.

He's grown quiet, and I take a page from his book and give his thigh a quick, reassuring squeeze under the table. He responds with a warm glance and the lopsided grin that makes me wish the girls were going to be out tonight.

I think it's our family dynamics that give Nate pause. There are three women to deal with. We are loud, exuberant, and often overly emotional, even by our standards. There's a part of me that wants to reassure him that it's not as bad as it could be. When the twins started their periods together, for example, now that was a hormonal roller coaster. If Nate is still here in a few years, it'll be my turn for the hormonal chaos. I don't say anything, though. Nate and I are too new, no matter how much I feel as though I've known him forever. And this allows the guilt over being happy with Nate to rear its unwelcome mug again. Because if I'd known Nate forever, where does that put Tom, who's been gone six years this month?

"You're quiet," Nate says, dipping an unagi roll into a tiny bowl of soy sauce. My mind can't help but wander back to the eel weir, to Jacob's Run. To two victims.

"Me?" I wave his observation away. "It's been a day full of…surprises."

"The shock of your mother being shot can't help."

"Yeah, Grandma's a badass." Ava chews thoughtfully on her salad. "Mom, you went to war and back and didn't get shot. Grandma takes a hit here in Stonebridge. Wild."

"She didn't get shot, she got grazed. Odds are that the bullet wasn't meant for her but that she was the unintended victim." Does everyone else hear how unconvinced I am? My chopsticks shake as I pluck at my California roll.

"It was at the same place the chiropractor dude got shot," Lily says.

"Hank Price. The victim has a name, Lily."

"Sorry, Mom." She's sincere and I regret that the topic of murder is anywhere near our family dinner table. I'm worried about my mother, too, but don't want to get the girls wound up. Mom will be fine, it's a matter of when. I suspect the wound will heal faster than the mental trauma.

"You should be sorry, Sister." Ava shoves Lily with her shoulder. Lily shoots Ava a vicious glare before smiling wide-mouthed, revealing her masticated food.

"Sexy. You kiss your boyfriend with that mouth?" Ava asks. She barely finishes her query before they both erupt in a fit of giggles.

I put my last piece of sushi in my mouth, and set my chopsticks down. They're ebony lacquer with teeny tiny cherry blossoms painted on the sides. I found them in an open-air flea market in Misawa, Japan. I notice Nate's empty dish. "Did you get enough to eat?"

"Plenty."

"Want to—"

"Go up on the roof?" He's read my mind. Except it's a balcony, not the roof. I nod, wipe my mouth with my napkin, and push back from the table.

"Girls, you have cleanup. Put Ralph in his cage if you're not going to be in the same room as him."

"We know, Mom." Ava doesn't roll her eyes but her tone assures me that she's not overly stressed about current events. Lily grabs another piece of pizza.

"Bye." Ralph speaks from his cage-top perch in the living room, visible from the kitchen since I pulled down a wall when we renovated before moving in last summer.

Nate and I make our way out of the kitchen and I stop to give Ralph a quick kiss on his birdie beak.

"Awww." Ralph's pouring it on thick, trying to keep me in the same room.

"Sorry, buddy. We're not leaving but you're not coming upstairs with Mommy right now."

Once we're on the balcony, I light the citronella oil lamps and sit on the glider seat, patting the cushion next to mine. "I missed you."

Nate doesn't wait for a second invitation. He sits beside me, his warmth an immediate balm to my overwrought nerves. The squeak the glider makes at his weight comforts me almost as much as the kiss he levels on my lips.

"We're getting into quite the routine, aren't we?" I smile, gazing into his eyes. They're crinkled around the edges, like mine.

"Indeed." He stretches his arm across the back of the seat, and I lean my head on his shoulder. His fingers find my hair and massage the base of my head.

"Mmm. You have no idea how much I need your magic fingers. My muscles are very cranky today."

"You're worried about your mom." A soft kiss brushes the top of my head.

"I am. I was. I mean, she's going to be fine, once she's over the shock. I won't rest easy until I know this so-called researcher was the real deal. But even if he's legit"—I straighten up and look at Nate—"it doesn't take away from the fact she was hit at the same place Hank was. I need to go see it again, walk the path alongside Jacob's Run."

His brows knit. "It's not a place that one gets shot at by accident, Angel. The terrain on that portion of the hiking trail is hilly, and there are a lot of tree roots and boulders. Whoever fired those two shots meant to. There have already been two victims. I don't want you to be number three."

"Wait a minute, have you been out there since Hank was shot?"

"Mach and I use that path several times a week. As long as it's not icy or too muddy. Or buggy, which early in the day it isn't. I know it well."

"You didn't answer my question, Nate."

"Yes, I went out there after you found Hank. Did you think I wouldn't?"

"No." While what Nate told my family about being in international shipping before he switched careers to become Stonebridge's sexiest barista is true, he's shared other parts of his former life with me. After he retired from the merchant marines, he spent five years as a logistics contractor for the government. Which meant he was hired to move any number of items, often classified in nature, around the globe. On paper, Nate's résumé reads as if he's lived in New York City for the twenty-five years before he moved to Stonebridge, when in fact he's better traveled than I am. Besides sharing globe-trotting backgrounds, we both are naturally inquisitive.

"What if you or Mach had been hurt, Nate?"

He shakes his head. "We're not the shooter's targets.

Whoever got Hank wanted to get him."

"Then how do you explain my mother being shot?"

"I can't, unless the killer made an error and missed."

"Unlikely if the shooter who killed Hank is the sharp-shooter Trinity says they are. Trinity's going to close off the entire area surrounding the weir, but I don't know how much of the walking path. Stay away from the weir, Nate. Don't even walk on the path next to it."

"Babe, I'll do as you ask, but I really don't believe Mach or I are targets. I've been here for a short time, and I don't have my thumb on Stonebridge politics. If there's someone out there who's willing to kill over that pile of rocks—no offense to your mother or her committee—then they're going after the people who have a vested interest in the weir. Such as your mother and Hank, not the average dude walking his dog. Plus, Mach and I walk earlier in the day. Both of the shots happened later."

"Yeah, it was way later than when you and Mach go." It still drove cold spikes of fear through my heart to think of anyone I loved being a killer's target.

"Did you or Bryce see a lot of people on the trails the day Hank was killed?"

"I wasn't paying close enough attention to recall. There were quite a few folks present where we got into the water, but I don't remember seeing anyone on the path. I was all about relaxing on the water, frankly. Bryce and I noticed that one loud sound we assumed was a firework, but now I wonder if it was the gunshot. They're usually very different sounds, for the most part, but like I said, we were chilling on the water and I wasn't expecting to hear a gunshot." Although my body had reacted as if it had.

"No, I'm sure you weren't. Listen, I'm no expert in crime solving, but I think I'm getting to know you well enough to see that you're beating yourself up here. Angel, babe, if it was a gunshot you heard, there's still nothing you could have done for Hank. The shot killed him, right?"

I nod. "Yes. It had to be instant, too, as he didn't bleed a lot and there were indications he'd died immediately. The autopsy backs that up. My head knows the truth, but my heart isn't listening."

"Awww, babe." He kisses me, and it deepens for long moments. Eventually I pull back and snuggle against him, allowing his warmth to keep the scary thoughts at bay.

We push the glider as the darkness settles in and makes the scent of Mrs. Carver's roses all the headier. Frogs, crickets, and cicadas compete for the loudest noise, and the *whooing* of a nearby owl adds to the ambience.

I won't figure out who killed Hank tonight, no matter how hard I think about it. So I try to let it go and enjoy being next to Nate.

Not a difficult task.

Chapter Seventeen

TRINITY GRINS AT me, the rising sun warming her cheekbones to a deep-amber glow. "This better be worth it, my friend. I could be catching up on my beauty rest."

"It's worth it already! Look at us, early birds and all that." My enthusiasm makes Trinity laugh. "Thanks for agreeing to meet this early, and out here, instead of in the shop."

"No problem. It's a good break from my usual routine, too. And no way do I want you flying that drone anywhere that puts you at risk."

Standing at the start of the Jacob's Run hiking path, we're both dressed in long but light pants and long-sleeved shirts. No matter the temperature, ticks are plentiful in Pennsylvania and so is Lyme disease.

Last night when I couldn't sleep, I texted Trinity right before midnight and asked if she'd be willing to meet at Jacob's Run. I need her permission to bring the drone back later, and I want to know if there are any areas she'd like me to take a closer look at.

"Here, I'll scoot ahead." I take the lead on a narrow stretch of the well-worn path that runs parallel to the creek, but above the water by anywhere from two to twelve feet.

"There are a lot of through hikers out this morning." The scent of a couple bearing framed backpacks announces them before they turn the corner in front of us and pass. Not an unusual occurrence as AT hikers often go a few days between showers at various camping respites or from bathing in natural water.

"This is the busy time, right? If they're heading south, that is." Trinity falls back alongside me on a wider part of the path.

"Yeah." We pass a man with two large, leashed dogs who move aside to give us room.

"Thank you. Good doggies!" I smile at the two Labradors, and then catch back up to Trinity.

Hank's expression wasn't anything short of total surprise. He didn't see the bullet coming. "Can you tell me if anyone heard the shot that killed Hank?"

"No. No one noticed a gunshot or any similar sound. Which backs up your and Bryce's belief that you heard a firework. And gives us zero leads." The defeat in Trinity's tone is palpable.

"So they used a silencer. It's possible."

"Yes. And it explains why no one heard a shot when your mother was hit, either. The time of death can only be narrowed so far. Hank could have been killed any time between ten thirty a.m. and two p.m."

"Which means Verity was right." We stop and Trinity turns to look at me. "Besides Verity, and the murderer, I was the last one to see Hank alive."

"That doesn't mean you have to be the first one to figure out who did it, Angel." Trinity's words are fierce but her expression is resigned. "Can I say, and I'll never admit I did in fact say this, that I'm glad we've connected again?"

"So you're not upset that I'm a self-appointed volunteer investigator?"

"More like a pain-in-my-behind wannabe." Her grin flashes bright against her dark skin. "That's not fair. You lend your own expertise to a crime scene, and the investigation. But if anything happens to you, it's on me. The entire department would be gutted if a civilian suffered because she was doing what we're all trained to do."

"Well, it's not like I'm *un*trained."

"We've been through this before, girlfriend. Navy training and law enforcement methods are not the same."

"I'm not putting myself in dangerous situations."

"Says she who's walking the path near where two bullets have flown over."

"You win this one. So"—I waved my arm wide—"I thought I'd come here with my drone and fly it downriver to the weir, go over the creek bank on both sides."

"That's fine, but focus on upstream, the less-traveled spots between the end of the path at the parking lot and the

Prices' house. My team scoured the creek bank in front of their home, and of course adjacent the weir. It's possible we missed something in between."

"Though you doubt it," I say. Trinity backs her officers 100 percent, as any decent leader would. And she's justified in doing so. SPD is noted as the best in the county.

She sighs. "I do, honestly. But we need a break in the case. Far stranger things have happened than a civilian stumbling upon a vital clue." She air quotes "civilian" and gives me a wink.

I would love to be the one who breaks this case wide open.

Chapter Eighteen

WITH TRINITY'S OKAY to fly my drone over the murder scene, I tentatively plan to fly it tomorrow morning, weather permitting. An afternoon thunderstorm is predicted so today won't work.

I decide I'll need the most up-to-date map of Stonebridge to compare to my drone footage. An hour in my office spent searching every last real estate and satellite imagery map database yields zilch. The density of trees and shrubbery along Jacob's Run isn't giving me the topographic details I want.

I know who might be a big help in this area. I pick up my phone.

"Hi there, Angel," Mom answers on the first ring.

"How are you feeling, Mom?"

"Much better." Her voice sounds far away, distracted.

"Mom, are you driving?"

"It's just a quick trip to the police station, honey. Trinity wants me to meet with her and the head of the Penn State Anthropology Department. We're going to verify that the grad student—you know, the TA who fled the scene—was legit. Which I know he was, but Trinity needs proof. For her case." Mom's speech accelerates, and I imagine her foot getting heavier on the gas pedal, too.

"Mom, you were supposed to rest, remember? I would have driven you to the station."

"Rest from what? A brush burn? Please. And you have your own life to live."

"Well, I need a quick answer from you. When you needed maps of Jacob's Run, where did you go? The historical society?" I already know that I'm probably going to have to make a trek to the centuries-old cabin down on Main Street. It houses the Stonebridge Historical Society. I was hoping for a more recent land survey, though.

"Well, you have several options. The historical society does have some of the first sketches of Stonebridge, including the first street map. But if you really want detail, and to see the changes through the years, you have to go to town hall. It's in their archival department. But if you want to save time, there's an easier way." Mom's passionate about every itty-bitty detail of Stonebridge history. Since retiring from teaching English at Stonebridge High School, she's morphed her passion for Shakespeare into studying Stonebridge. It's a blessing and a curse. I'm trying to avoid the curse part—learning about details I'll never retain nor care about—as my time is short, and Hank's murder still isn't solved.

"What's the easiest way, Mom?"

"Why, the library, of course. They keep a copy of everything stored by town hall, except it's all digital. Which is okay but I have to tell you there's nothing like holding a piece of paper that someone drew a map on two hundred years ago. I'm sorry but a computer screen or printout just isn't the same."

I've already left my office and I'm moving toward the front. I stop at the counter and smile at Lily. The shop's empty, but judging from the tour bus marked PENNSYLVANIA TREASURE TOURS, and the sportily dressed passengers debarking, it won't be quiet for much longer.

"Thanks, Mom. Let me know how it goes at the police station. Talk to you later. Love you."

"Love you, too." Mom sounds a bit more energetic.

Lily patiently waits for me to tell her what she's no doubt overheard. "I'm heading to the library. I'll be right back. Text me if it gets crazy."

"Mom, I can handle it. What's at the library? Nate?" She grins.

"Not Nate." But it wouldn't be a bad idea to stop in at Latte Love after I figure a few things out. If the library has the information I need.

I want to determine exactly how far the Prices' property is from where Hank, and my mother, was shot.

THE STONEBRIDGE LIBRARY is housed in a former flour

factory. The edifice is a tribute to stone masonry no longer practiced in this part of the world, which is a sad loss. Limestone underlies the vast farm fields surrounding our town, and is the bane of every residential gardener who wants to dig up a new flower bed without the help of commercial equipment. In fact, it's not a stretch to say limestone helps keep my brother-in-law Brad in business, as evidenced by his array of groundbreaking equipment. Breaking up the massive boulders takes more than muscle—it requires professional knowledge, power tools, and commercial-grade landscaping equipment.

When the library was built for flour milling in the early nineteenth century, the settlers used what they had available and the result is that the original building still stands, and is where I'm entering. There have been two major additions since the county purchased the building in 1952 with library funds. It's modern and provides our town with the latest and greatest in multimedia needs while retaining the essence of history that keeps Stonebridge on the map.

As I pass through the lobby to the information desk, my gaze catches on a wall display. The framed photos of previous head librarians with their names and dates of service are striking, as they go back to 1835, over a century before the library was in this building and was run out of a private home.

My focus narrows in on the photo of a pleasant woman with a winning smile. The engraved words under read

MABEL SMITH MOORE, HEAD LIBRARIAN 2012–2022. My heart squeezes with commiserate sadness for Kevin Moore. I'm glad he's taking care of himself by getting a job with Nate. Being around people was the best antidote to my grief, not that anything but time really eases it.

I move on to the information desk and ask about the historical documents. The multimedia specialist is knowledgeable, and within minutes, I'm wearing white gloves and staring at a map drawn in 1935. Jacob's Run and its unique triple S route are clear, as is the area between town and the water, which today holds entire neighborhoods up to where the tree line begins. The current hiking/walking/running path was installed as part of the Publics Work Act of 1933, and as I look at the map, I think I make out where the Prices' property is. There's no indication of the two cabins that Verity mentioned but the spot I see has to be her property.

Except.

Verity stated that their property led to the path, after a quarter mile or so. According to this map, the path goes right along their property line before turning west, toward the Appalachian Trail.

I see the eel weir penciled in, and instead of being out of view of the Prices' land, it's a direct line of sight. I'll need the drone's photos to be certain, but I estimate it's a straight line of three hundred yards at the most. A stretch for the average hunter, sure, but doable by a skilled marksman with the most up-to-date equipment. Including a silencer.

I kick myself for not taking a walk to the back of the Prices' property when I was there, and I also wonder if she didn't encourage me to leave the pool area because she didn't want me to see just how close she is to the weir.

It's impossible to tell from the water, and land while on foot, what's what as far as properties and houses go, especially when it's all obscured by woods and underbrush.

But one thing is strikingly clear. Verity Price has a clear shot to the weir from her land.

BACK AT THE shop, I work on my inventory in the storage room. I had great sales numbers for last year's holiday merchandise, but there are still a few items left over that we can sell this coming season. It's not easy to think about Hanukkah and Christmas in the middle of summer, but it's de rigueur for retail.

It took me several months to be able to walk back in here without seeing the dead body of Frannie Schrock on the floor. I still think of her, and send up a prayer, but I no longer feel as if I'm walking into a death chamber of sorts. Of course, it hasn't been a year yet and I haven't had to relive the same time of year. I imagine Halloween will make me reconsider.

I'm happy to see that there's plenty of room for the

German and Italian carved and resin nativity figurines that I'd like to feature. And this year I'll add in three more styles of menorahs, as the ceramic, wooden, and silver ones sold out.

My next focus is on Diwali. I noticed many Stonebridge homes went all out with colorful lights for the festival, and I want to make sure I support local customers the best I can. I've found an Indian mercantile company that specializes in brightly colored linens such as table runners and napkins, as well as lanterns. I placed the order back in January and the box arrived yesterday. I've been so buried in trying to make heads or tails of Hank Price's murder that it's still unopened. My box cutter makes a satisfying click as I pop up a fresh blade. Finally, some quiet time to sample the goods.

"Hey, Angel."

"Whoa!" I jump back, arms wide, and the razor tool goes flying, hits the hardwood floor, and skitters to a stop at Trinity's foot.

"You okay?" Her hands are up, palms facing.

"Yes, I'm fine."

Trinity's disbelieving expression is quickly masked by what I think of as her detective face. That's when I notice the tall man next to her. And he must be tall if he towers over Trinity, who's nothing under five foot ten.

"Angel, I thought I'd bring Professor Anthony Watkins in to meet you."

I step around the box and dust my hands off on my

pants before I offer my hand. We shake.

"Professor, meet Angel Warren."

"Please, call me Tony."

Trinity looks at me. "Can we get a cup of coffee here? We'd go to the coffee shop, but I'm afraid it might be hard to hear ourselves in there this time of day."

"Of course." I totally hear between her lines. Trinity wants this conversation to be private. I escort them into my office and motion for them to each take one of the visitor chairs while I get the beverages going.

"Coffee or tea, Tony?"

"Black tea if you have it."

"Same. With oat milk. Can you froth it and make it a tea latte?" Trinity must really want this to be an in-depth discussion.

"That's a fancy order for an office coffee nook." Professor Watkins—Tony—has a teasing note in his voice that makes me smile. I sneak a peek at Trinity, and from the glow of her cheeks, I'd say she's not immune to Tony's charm.

"We aim to please in Stonebridge. So I take it you're from State College?"

"That's right."

"Professor Watkins is the Anthropology Department's archaeology chair."

"Trinity, please, it's Tony." If his voice gets any lower, I'm afraid I'll need to duck out and leave them alone for a bit. When the drinks are finished and we're all settled, me behind my desk, I check Tony's left hand. No rings, but of course, that's not a hard-and-fast rule these days. He could still be married, or in a partnership. But it's hard not to immediately think of the romantic possibilities as he's hotter than all get-out, as in he could have walked off a movie screen. And Trinity's always been beautiful, but the years and experience look particularly good on her.

"Angel, I told Tony"—her breath catches a bit there—"that you're my trusted friend and that you were the first witness of the crime scene."

"Other than the murderer." Although the shooter could have been far enough away to not have ever seen more than Hank dropping.

"Was the research assistant legit?" I look from Trinity to Tony.

Tony nods. "Absolutely. Fred Unser is literally my right-hand grad student in the department. He had a panic attack and reacted by taking off. I'm so sorry about any confusion."

"He must have been terrified."

Tony nods. "He was, but he did call it in to the police before he kept going."

"I'm glad he wasn't hurt." My stomach flips at how close he and my mother came to suffering much worse than her bullet graze.

"You okay, Angel?" Trinity reads me well.

"I'm good. It's been an interesting week so far, though."

"We're only at hump day, girlfriend," Trinity says.

"Olivia—your mother, Angel, right?—is a familiar face in our offices. She's very persistent." Tony's wide smile brightens his face. Dark-brown eyes flash with enthusiasm.

"Yes, well, Mom's very passionate about the weir and its place in local history. Do you believe it's authentically ancient, Tony?" I ask.

He shrugs. "I'm a scientist first, dreamer second. We have to find a remnant of the weir—a wooden piece—so that we can carbon-date it. The stones themselves are definitely ancient, as is all of the limestone that literally litters this part of Pennsylvania. We're ranked as the rockiest state of the Appalachian Trail for a reason."

"I hear it from the southbound through-hikers who stop in my store all the time. They come off the trail via the Jacob's Run path and shower at the facility in Stone Cliff Park. Many wander through town to get a real meal and search for souvenirs before getting back on the AT."

"The post office is right down the street so it's a perfect locale," Trinity adds. "Anything they buy in town can be shipped to their permanent residence." It's not like her to be forthcoming with someone she's just met. She's a collector of information by her job description. In fact, it's fair to say Trinity's showing her most sparkly self to the professor. I wonder if she realizes that she's giving me a lot of ammunition to tease her with later.

"And many stores, like mine, offer free shipping on purchases." I lean forward. "Tony, it's really important that we figure out if the weir is Native American or not. As you've found out, and unfortunately your grad student learned the hard way, there are folks around here who don't want any part of an archaeological dig in Jacob's Run. The thought of even more tourists showing up by the busload to see what they view as no more than a pile of rocks is anathema to them."

"That's understandable. I'm not a local but I wouldn't want that for the weir, either." Tony leans back in his chair. "I can't tell you how many sites have been overrun by tourists in the past several decades. The human interest is natural and needed, to keep the projects funded. But it's alarming to the folks in my business. We aim to preserve the past so that we can study it."

"Yet if you prove it's of historical value, we can't keep it quiet, can we?"

"No, but if you emphasize how difficult it would be to drain Jacob's Run in order to isolate the weir, it will go a long way in keeping it from becoming commercial. First things first, though. As of this moment there's no evidence that the weir is older than the colonists who settled here."

"How much time do you need to find proof, Tony?"

"If the weather reports are accurate, the water's going to be at its lowest point over the next two weeks. It's also summer break, and I have several students who are available to do the work. But I'm not comfortable after what's happened. I can't put anyone else in danger. Not until you catch the shooter." Tony looks at Trinity with complete confidence. As he should. She's the best in the detective biz in these parts. But I sense his confidence has more to do with the chemistry I sense between them.

"So there won't be an answer until the case is solved," I say.

"Except"—Tony flashes a grin at Trinity—"I'm personally interested in this. There's a wealth of research opportunities in this single spot if we can determine the weir's age. With your town's and local police department's approval, I plan to begin the excavation myself. I'll need a police or private security detail. One guard is plenty. I've found that the presence of a person holding a loaded weapon is deterrent enough. If you solve the crimes in time, I can bring in the students."

"The professor has operated in dangerous foreign locations, on other digs," Trinity expounds.

"I never thought of archaeologic sites as being places you'd need protection for unless there's treasure involved."

Tony nods. "You're correct. I have to admit, this would be the first site I've had where someone's been randomly murdered, another person shot at."

I don't think there's anything random about the Jacob's Run shooter. Neither does Trinity, I'm certain.

"Don't you live in State College? How will you manage the logistics?" Would he commute two hours one way?

"Detective Colson has graciously offered her guesthouse."

I know my eyes are wide as I look at Trinity. "Your guesthouse?"

"My dad's." She shoots me a warning glare before she smiles at Tony. "It's a converted carriage house on my parents' property."

"Perfect." He drains his mug. "Thank you for the coffee, Angel. I'd like to get going as soon as possible."

We all stand.

"It was nice meeting you."

"And you. Please, check out the store before you go."

Tony walks out into the retail area to browse, and I grab Trinity's elbow. She turns to face me but her gaze lingers on Tony...down to his snug-fitting jeans.

"What's going on?"

"I brought him by as a courtesy to you. I thought you'd be relieved to know that your mother was working with a student researcher and not anyone more nefarious."

"Yes, I am happy to know that. Before I forget, I have to let you in on something." I tell her what I found in the library.

"Don't you think my officers have already figured that out?" Her annoyance breaks through her thinning patience.

"Of course I know that, and I swear I'm not trying to overstep."

"Tell me, then. What are you thinking?"

"I think Verity Price could have shot her husband without a problem. She could have shot him, and made it back to her place, before Bryce and I ever found him."

Trinity stills, and I know she's already thought this theory through.

"You're right, she could have." Trinity stares at me. "Good job."

Relief pulses through my tight chest, and I suck in a deep breath. We're getting closer. Aren't we?

Chapter Nineteen

TRINITY'S NEXT WORDS squelch my hope that I'm on a path to solving the murder. "That's always a possibility, except how do you explain your mom's shooter? Because the direction of the shot was on the other side of the water from where Hank was shot, according to the ballistics reports. There's no way to be certain that it was even the same gun, because we haven't found the bullet that grazed your mom. And Verity has an alibi for the time your mother was shot at."

"What's her alibi?"

"She was picking out flowers for the funeral. The florist—your sister—confirms."

"Huh. And you're positive the second shot was from a different location?" I ask.

"Absolutely."

"I'll focus on that with the drone. You're still okay with it, with me flying it?"

"You already have my official permission, Angel."

"You won't regret it." I grin.

"I'd better not." Trinity returns my smile.

"One more thing, about Verity, even though you've ruled her out as a suspect. I know I mentioned it before, but her behavior was off when I was there. It's not how I remember reacting to Tom's passing, not at all. She seemed so detached from it, except for when she broke down a couple of times."

"Tom's passing and Hank's murder are apples and oranges, my friend. Murder takes it out of you with zero warning, and the violence of it is always traumatic, no matter what the means of death is." Trinity's observation stops me short. She's the only person who could say this to me without hurting my feelings.

"You're right. I've been projecting my stuff onto Verity. Probably not the hallmark character asset of a good investigator, huh?"

She smiles. "You're very objective with most situations, and you definitely have superior observation abilities. And your ability to connect the dots is superior. Which is why I appreciate your input on the case, as long as—"

"As long as I don't overstep into the dangerous or not-my-expertise category. I get it. Sorry to interrupt you, by the way." I cross my arms across my chest. "So, the professor. Why did you really stop by, Trin?"

Trinity gives me a tiny smile. "He's single. And attractive. Did you notice?"

"I may have." I grin. "I'm impressed, Trin. You're letting your inner sensuous woman out. It's not like you to get all aflutter over a guy, even if he could be a movie double for Idris Elba."

"He's been professional to the nth degree. He didn't have to drive out here, of course, but insisted. Accountability for his team's action, or inaction, is important to him," she says.

"A responsible, mature, sexy man. How did you figure out he's single so quickly?" I don't want to admit I checked for a ring.

"He came to the station and asked to see me. I was waiting for him, as he'd told my officer that he'd be driving from State College to Stonebridge this morning and planned to stop at the department first. We spent the morning driving around town, so that he could get the lay of the land. He mentioned that he's single. When I realized that he's dead serious about staying here until he finds what he needs to carbon-date the weir, I immediately thought of my father's vacation rental."

"It's not already booked for the summer? That's surprising."

"It's luck, actually. An artist couple rented it through August but they just broke up and left. Dad's got it cleaned out and ready to go, and I'm the good daughter who found him a quieter occupant."

"Quiet, eh? That could change, depending on who he makes friends with around here." I laugh, unable to stop even at Trinity's sheepish expression.

"Hush. This stays between us, right?" Trinity unnecessarily asks.

"Of course. It's all under the heading of the investigation, right?" I hold up my left pinky finger and Trinity responds the same. We link fingers and shake once, twice, three times.

It's as though we never had the twenty-five-year gap in our friendship.

AFTER TRINITY AND Tony leave, I get back to work in the storage room. Maybe getting into a headspace where I'm doing a repetitive task—like stocking shelves—will help shake out some clues I've overlooked.

After an hour of placing vibrant pink, blue, yellow, and red lanterns in neat rows, I decide it's time to break for lunch. It'll be a quick meal, as it's later than I realized. I usually just run upstairs for a bite, but I need to get out of the building. Fresh air and a change of surroundings helps me think, too.

"I'm heading out to lunch," I tell Ava at the counter. She relieved Lily while I was elbow deep in holiday decor.

"Will you bring me back a cold brew, Mom? Pretty please?"

"Sure, honey. It might be a bit, I need to eat first. Did you have lunch?"

"I finished the pizza from last night."

"Great. I'll be back."

"Bye."

As soon as I exit the air-conditioned store, I'm struck by the wall of moist heat that defines a south central Pennsylvania summer. Latte Love is to the left, down a few blocks, but they don't have much in the way of meals. More like baked goods, savory and sweet. A cold salad or veggie wrap sounds more appealing in this heat. I turn right on my way to Le Quaint Café. I don't judge the loose interpretation of the French language. Not too much, anyway. Not everyone has had the privilege of being stationed in Belgium. It hits me right now, on Main Street with the asphalt baking in the intense heat, that I'm happier than I can remember being in a long while.

It's interesting to me that I don't miss any of the exotic places I've lived. I miss the girls at whatever age they were at each duty station. Of course any memory of when Tom was alive can trigger a pang of longing. But overall, I'm doing the blooming where I planted myself. I've figured out that the motto I adopted since going off to Annapolis as an eighteen year old still holds. I can be happy wherever I am. Home is where the heart is, and my chosen home after so much change is Stonebridge.

It's too hot to sit under the blue-and-white-striped awning under which several tables sit, surrounded by customers who are all at least twenty if not thirty years younger. Being capable of my own personal hormonal heat wave makes a cooler venue ideal. I say a silent prayer of thanks for air conditioning as I enter the café, giving my eyes a second to adjust. The chalkboard sign instructs me to choose my own seat, which shouldn't be difficult. The lunch crowd has emptied, and several tables are available. I scan the room for a quiet spot. That's when I see Verity, seated at a table in the far corner, her arms waving about as she talks to Eloise.

My stomach growls. I need to eat. I shouldn't walk over to the two besties; it'd be close to rude since I know what Verity's going through and spoke to her only yesterday.

It's a phenomenon, truly, how my legs carry me to their table as if my appetite is already sated.

"Hey, ladies."

Verity stops midsentence and gapes at me. Eloise's expression is calm, her seemingly constant state of serenity evident. She smiles at me with genuine affection.

"Angel! You two know each other, right?" She looks at Verity, back at me. By all appearances, Eloise never shared our conversation with Verity.

"Are you kidding? I'm in Shop 'Round the World more than I'm in my office," Verity says. She's regained her composure and her face, while pale, offers a welcoming smile. "Why don't you join us, Angel?"

"Oh no, I'm grabbing a late lunch. I really just want to say hello."

"Nonsense. We haven't placed our orders yet. Sit." Eloise gives me an offer I can't refuse. Maybe Verity will shed more light on the case here than I'd ever be able to draw from her on my own.

We order drinks and look at the menu after the server leaves.

"I am surprisingly hungry." Verity ogles the menu.

"No surprise when you haven't eaten since Saturday, I'd say." Eloise peers over her readers, the same shade of violet as her logo and the lotus printed on her tank top. "You haven't, have you?"

"It's all been such a shock." She closes the menu. "No, I haven't had much more than peanut butter and crackers in the evenings. They line my stomach for the bottle of wine." A sad excuse for a smile crosses her face, and it's heartbreaking to see her try to make us laugh in the midst of her pain.

Or it would be tragic, if I didn't still think she was the prime suspect in Hank's murder, lack of evidence notwithstanding.

"I remember not having a regular meal for weeks after Tom died. Be kind to yourself." My commiseration is genuine, but the tug of guilt at knowing it's also manipulative way to get information out of Verity reminds me that I'm once again balanced on an ethical tightrope.

"Verity, Angel is probably the best person you can talk to about everything. She's gone through it," Eloise says.

"You've been so kind to me, Angel. You make me feel not so alone," Verity says.

"I'm glad I could help. I haven't gone through a murder,

though. But becoming widowed well before my time? Yes," I say.

"You have children, don't you?" Verity asks, her gaze wistful.

"Yes, twin girls."

"At least your husband left you a living legacy. I have nothing from Hank except a pile of debts." She slams her mouth shut. Maybe Verity meant that comment for Eloise.

"Debts you can pay off, or something worse?" I press.

The server brings our drinks and takes our food orders. Verity and Eloise are each having the daily special, grilled eggplant with aioli sauce on a spinach wrap. I opt for the salad Niçoise. We agree to share a large order of *pommes frites avec mayonnaise*.

Verity leans in close after the server departs. "I don't want to drag you into my personal nightmare, Angel. Eloise already knows all of the sordid details. And she trusts you, so I do, too. The fact is that Hank is a gambler. *Was* a gambler. He was in recovery for it since right after we married. But he's had some slips over the past couple of years. Or that's what I thought. Turns out he was probably involved in illegal gambling and must owe some really bad characters a pile of cash. There's no other explanation for how our money has disappeared."

"I'm sorry, Verity." I sip my iced tea. I've got to let Trinity know about this. "Have you told Detective Colson? The police would have a handle on gambling rings in the area, I'd expect."

"Yes, I told Detective Colson, and she said they'd check it out. It doesn't matter, though, as far as my credit score is concerned. Hank was taking money from every single one of our accounts to gamble, and now there's nothing left for me to pay the regular bills with. Even our mortgage is behind."

"But only by a month, and you'll get that fixed soon enough. You bring in enough with your practice to keep you afloat, right?" Eloise says, patting Verity's forearm.

"That's what I thought yesterday. Now that I've spoken to a real CPA, I'm not so sure." Just like when we were poolside, tears pour down Verity's cheeks and she buries her face in her hands. My heart twists like the lemon on my tea glass. I'm trying to stay detached, to mentally collect all the facts, but Verity's pain is acute.

"It's brave of you to go to a professional right away. A lot of grieving people wait—it's so much to face in the beginning. Having the numbers in black and white, all the facts, is your only way out of this." I send up a silent thanks that Tom and I took care of all of the paperwork, from power of attorney to wills to life insurance policies, shortly after his tragic diagnosis. I never faced the financial havoc Verity claims she is. "What about life insurance? Savings?"

She shakes her head. "I had no idea before now, but Hank cashed in all of our life insurance policies within the last six months. They were whole-life and our investment vehicles for retirement. We were going to retire when we were fifty, to be full-time parents to the high school age kids we never were able to have." She hiccups between her words and sobs. Eloise grabs more napkins from the empty table next to us.

"Here, honey." Eloise puts her arm around Verity's shoulders, murmurs quiet words of comfort.

My fingers are itching to pull the old-school notebook and pen I always carry in my shoulder bag but writing down Verity's suffering is *tres* not apropos.

"I may seem like just another retail store owner, but I happen to have been in charge of the budget for a large navy project at my last duty station. You're going to get through this, Verity."

"Thank you."

"Do you want to go over what you know so far?"

She nods. "That would be a relief, to be honest. I can't talk about this with my parents. I'm an only child and they've always been so protective. They never wanted me to marry Hank in the first place. And Hank's family isn't an option. We've been estranged from them for a long while."

I pull out my notepad. "I'm going to write down everything we talk about and give it to you, okay?" I'm definitely doing this for my own motives but there's nothing wrong with helping out a recent widow. And if I'm proven wrong, if Verity didn't kill Hank, then it will be a plain old good deed.

"Honey, why don't you list out all of your assets," Eloise

says.

"Here." Verity pulls out her phone and taps, swipes, taps. "I already made a list of everything for the attorney. I have the business, the house, our three cars, my secret stash."

"Secret stash?" I ask.

"It's not a lot, but it's money my mother told me to always have on hand that my spouse can't get to. Just in case I have to leave in a hurry."

"Your mother is a wise woman," I say.

"She sure is. The nicest man can become a monster with little warning." Eloise speaks with such authority I rack my memory for anything about her and her husband, or past husbands. But we've only become reacquainted since I moved back and we're not besties by any stretch.

"Hank wasn't a monster, but his gambling sickness sure made him act like one, judging from all the money that's gone." Verity puts the phone on the table, raises her hands to the base of her throat in the primal signal for distress. "Can you imagine, he literally drained us dry?"

"But you have other assets. First, the mortgage. Can you cover it with your monthly earnings?"

She nods. "I can. And I can make most of the utilities. But I can't afford all the extras. The lawn service, pool service, my housekeeper." She starts to weep again. "Poor Elizabeth. Cleaning our home is one of her biggest accounts. What is she going to do? She has kids to feed and clothe."

"It'll be okay. Maybe you can work something out with

her in the short term." Eloise soothes with her voice and her arm, wrapped around Verity again. She gives her a quick squeeze then backs away. "And you don't have to decide everything right this minute."

"Eloise is right. You have some time."

"Not really. The bank is going to forfeit on the mortgage in two weeks if I can't come up with the back payments. I know that with my client load I have the cashflow to handle the monthly bills, but I don't have all I need to bring it out of the red. And I'm just talking about the house and utilities. Add in the business and all I can see is debt up to my ears."

"What did the lawyer and CPA say?"

"They're working to buy me more time to get solvent. And to protect me from any other gambling debt I'm not yet aware of. It's not unusual for a gambler to run up debt at a casino, and other legal gambling places, before resorting to illegal gambling and backdoor loans."

"You've been through this with Hank how many times before?"

Verity shakes her head. "He only slipped once before, early on in our relationship. Then he got the help he needed. Hank's the one who encouraged me to learn about the addiction and the signs I should be aware of in case he ever slipped. I just never believed he'd go off the wagon. I mean, why did he? We had such a good life together."

My widow's heart breaks for Verity's pain but my quieter self observes that it wasn't as great a marriage as Verity's claiming, not with an active gambler lying to her. Because that's what addiction does. It creates liars out of otherwise wonderful people. I saw it firsthand when I was in leadership positions that involved recommending a junior officer or sailor for rehab or, when that failed, permanent discharge.

"Verity, can I ask you another question?"

"What?"

"Did you and Hank purposefully want the community to think that you both saw patients? Because only you did, right?"

Verity stills, her face grows paler than the ashen it's been since Hank's murder. "That, yes...yes, it was the way we ran our business. Once Hank moved to Pennsylvania, we made a decision as a couple that one of us would practice chiropractics while the other ran the business. It's worked out well for us. We never intended to hoodwink anyone about it, if that's what you're getting at. It's not like there was anything to hide. I've built a loyal client base over the years and couldn't have done it without Hank's help."

What's that line from Shakespeare about protesting a bit too much?

If Hank and Verity didn't intend to deceive their customers, they sure went to lengths to keep it quiet. And how smart was it leaving Hank, a compulsive gambler, in charge of the finances? Sure, he'd been on the wagon for years, at least that's what Verity thinks. But facts are facts. Verity's accounts are in a mess caused by Hank.

I don't comment as Eloise and Verity hash out Verity's financial chaos. Taking notes as they talk is a good excuse to observe and listen.

Verity is awfully willing to open up about her financial woes, but she's not being transparent enough for me to remove her from my suspect list. She lied by omission about all of this—letting the general public assume Hank practiced, too, Hank's gambling addiction, and who knows what else? She hasn't been up front with me, or with Trinity.

And wouldn't revealing her financial mess be a perfect misdirect?

Chapter Twenty

I USED THE rest of Thursday after the lunch with Verity and Eloise to finish the inventory, in between retail shifts. On Friday I arise early, and instead of my usual coffee on the balcony with Ralph, I throw on shorts, a tank, ball cap, and water shoes. Nate's agreed to help me with my drone reconnaissance mission.

I drive out to Stone Cliff Park, only ten minutes from downtown. It's only half past six but there are already several people about. Runners of all kinds including a pack of parents pushing jogging strollers—the kind with the bigger wheels for just this purpose—as well as all varieties of hikers, walkers, and bicyclists. A wide half-mile path surrounds a grassy expanse. Inside the path is an inviting playground made entirely of recycled materials; a fenced-in, off-leash dog park; and a small skate park. Park benches line the entire loop, offering appealing views of either Jacob's Run or the foothills of the Appalachians.

My eyes don't waste any time on the people I'm in the midst of, not once I spot the tall silver-haired man with the wolflike dog. Nate and Mach are side by side at the water fountain, where Mach is lapping water from the ground-level doggie fountain. Nate's smile is morning sunshine and a warm hug in one.

As I approach my guys—I'm possessive, just a bit— Nate's gaze sweeps over me, stops on the drone, which is large compared to the average neighborhood toy. His eyes widen and he chuckles. "If that's the kind of drone you fly, I can't wait until you take us up for a real flight."

"I will, soon enough." I mean it. As much as I've enjoyed my solo getaways, it will be a pure joy to take Nate up. Mach, at 110 pounds, is still up for discussion. A lot of dogs enjoy flying but Mach is very large and very vociferous. As in, he howls. A lot.

"Owwoooooh." On cue, Mach greets me. I lean over and pucker my lips and am rewarded with a big lick on my cheek.

"You are undoing years of precision training," Nate deadpans.

"Hey, he's not jumping, and he wouldn't kiss me unless I invited him to."

"Only for you, Angel." Nate kisses me fully on the mouth. "I respect your previous career, but I do hope you know how to fly that thing. It's huge!"

I look at the top-level drone the girls surprised me with "from Santa." They thought I needed a hobby. Because opening my own international gift shop and flying small planes and helping Trinity solve murders isn't enough.

"I have no clue, to be honest. This is my first time with it. But the best part is that it has a camera. I used to fly with cameras aboard my helicopter. They were specially designed to take photos from a long way off. A drone can't be much different, other than its specs, right?"

Nate coughs and it suspiciously sounds like a cover for another chuckle. "A drone is not a combat aircraft. Is it out of line to remind you that you're not in a war zone?"

"No, but may I remind you that we've had two different people get shot at in this area in the past week?"

"Touché. You're right. I'm sorry." He stares at me, as if contemplating a puzzle. "How can I help? What would you like Mach and me to do?"

"I wish this wasn't about me getting more clues. I've wanted to spend time with you both all week. But until this case is solved…"

"It's okay, Angel. I'm happy with whatever time we have together. I always want more, of course, but we're not rookies in the relationship department. It's good that we're learning each other's routines before we—" He cuts himself off and I let it go. The butterflies in my stomach don't, though.

"I thought it would be fun to get some photos of Mach in the water to start with, to help me get familiar with the drone's controls. Also to give me something to reference for size. We can't get near the weir, though, or Trinity will have my hide. She's closed off that part of the creek, anyway."

"Mach's not going to let us get out of his sight, you know this," Nate says.

"Yes, I do. You're a sweet boy, Mach, aren't you?"

Mach's tail wags and he stares at me with complete doggie adoration. Mach's only recently decided to play like a retriever and—gasp!—get his humongous paws wet. He's taken to running into Jacob's Run when Nate and I go on walks together. Nate says Mach is showing off for me, that he doesn't go into the water without a lot of persuasion from Nate in the way of special treats from our local pet store, Cumberland Exotics.

"You should have seen him yesterday in that heat. He refused to go in the water, not even for his favorite peanut butter biscuits."

"Awww, your daddy's exaggerating, isn't he, buddy?" I stroke Mach's silky soft fur with my free hand, the other holding my phone. I've placed the drone on the ground for the moment. "I'll bet you were protecting him from a piranha, right?"

"Because northeastern America is known for its flesh-eating fish," Nate says.

I pick up the drone and we walk to a clear spot off the path.

"Can I ask what you're doing? I assume you're using an app?" Nate's never patronized me, ever, but I sense he's genuinely perplexed.

"Yes, I'm making sure the app on my phone is set, and

that the camera's working. It's my first time flying a drone."

He nods, absentmindedly stroking Mach's head. "Okay."

"Tell you what, why don't you and Mach go on ahead and I'll launch this puppy—no offense, Mach—and see what I get, okay? Head toward the third bend." I'm describing not the park's path but the creek-side route that goes for several miles. The third turn is a half mile downstream, and at the highest point. It's also the place where Hank fell into the water. "I'll catch up to you. Or at least the drone will."

Nate and Mach walk off at a quick clip. I get the drone up without a problem, and I'm comfortable maneuvering it. The app controls work like any other remote, and a drone is closer to a helicopter than the single engine plane I routinely fly these days.

The camera is giving me trouble, though. As in, I can't get it to focus. I'm not sure it's on. I walk in the same direction as Nate and Mach, but I can't make a lot of progress without being able to see where they are, specifically.

I'm about ten minutes into my mission when Mach's telltale *woof* reaches my ears. I glance at the path ahead of me and see he and Nate have returned.

"When I didn't see the drone, I thought we'd double back." Nate's in sync with me in so many ways.

"You didn't text—"

"Because I knew you already had enough to manage. I don't want to be the reason you'd crash a nice piece of tech."

He grins.

"It'd be my fault if I did." I sigh. "Yeah, I'm having issues. I can't get the camera to work."

"Can I give it a try?"

"You've worked with a drone before?" My controlling nature is usually kept in check since I'm no longer responsible for life-or-death activities, but it does rear its teeth every so often.

"Trust me?" He patiently waits for me to figure it out. Nate's a deliberate guy. Not one to do much of anything without first thinking it through.

"Yes, completely." I hand him my phone, and he gives me Mach's leash.

"Let's see…" With a few swipes and taps, Nate has the drone swoop and turn, then places it in a low hover over the water. Because Trinity shut down the creek, there aren't any kayakers or tubers.

"I'm impressed, Nate. Mach, do you see this? Your daddy's my hero."

Mach stands and wags his tail, ready to get going. Nate grunts. "Give me a sec before you put a cape on me."

I take the chance to look around, to try to imagine how it looked for Hank as he made his last walk with Moose, never suspecting a bullet would catapult him off the high creek bank, into the water right near the weir. Hank was an active member of the Stonebridge Historical Society; did he like to come this way regularly, to check out what he believed to be ancient? It makes sense that he'd use the path closer to his and Verity's house, but to come this far on each walk, which with the twists and turns, while only a quarter mile as the crow flies, is at least two miles from the Price house, seems unlikely to me. Especially during bad weather.

"Here we go." Nate tilts the phone so I can see the camera.

"How did you do that?"

"Ah, my previous profession."

"The part you don't talk about so much?"

He shrugs as he maneuvers the drone, works the camera focus, takes some photos. "It's nothing classified or confidential, if that's what you're asking. I found drones to be useful to account for larger shipments that would have otherwise eaten up a lot of my time to manually measure. And I used them when I was in the merchant marines, too. To be honest, I found drones best for mostly safety-related issues."

"And yet you failed to mention this earlier because…" I prompt.

"Investigating a murder is your gig; far be it from me to tell you how to do it. You're my warrior woman, Angel. I've learned it's best to never underestimate you." He's not being sarcastic and his eyes reflect sincerity. I give him a tight side-hug. I don't want to make him drop the phone or crash the drone.

"You're pretty amazing yourself," I say. "Are you sure we never met in our previous life?" Although I'd remember meeting Nate.

We both laugh over the phrase we've adopted to describe life before we met. Because it feels as though this is a completely different life. And we're finding a new life…together. With Mach and Ralph, of course.

For me, it's not just the new location, or the prospect of not having to move every few years. It's been a full turnaround from the responsibility I shouldered as a naval aviator to become a small business owner. Few people can relate to my military experience. Nate can, because as a boat captain he handled shipments for the government and military. He knows the kind of pressure I was under, and I have the same sense about his previous occupation. Logistics is the backbone of modern life, from consumer goods to combat gear.

Nate's shared that he views his move to Stonebridge and new career in small business entrepreneurship as more than a financial decision. He wanted to be part of a community, same as me.

"Do you mind operating the drone, Nate?"

"You'll allow me to?" he chides.

"Hey, don't blame me for being cautious. It wasn't inexpensive."

"Yeah, you can get cheaper drones that actually do quite a bit but this one is better for the battery life and photographic quality. You have the app set to download the images to your camera?"

"Yes, and they get backed up by my cloud storage service."

"You don't miss a beat, Angel Warren. Come back here." He doesn't take his gaze off the drone as he leans over for my kiss. I plant one on his cheek.

"We're getting more kissing than drone activity."

"Hmm. Tell me what you want captured with the camera, what you're looking for."

"I'm not sure yet, but I'll know it when I see it." Ideally I want to get photos or video of the entire area that encompasses the possible range of the rifle used to kill Hank, and possibly the same one that injured my mother. "Can you start with shots that take in the entirety of Jacob's Run, bank to bank, where the weir is?"

"Isn't the weir a half mile long?" he asks.

"No, that's the larger ones, like the one in the Susquehanna River. This weir is much smaller, so no more than a hundred yards. A football field."

He whistles. "That's still a big area. The drone will need to go pretty high. Did you get a license?"

"Are you kidding? You do know me, right? I'm Ms. Safety All the Way. Just ask the girls. I got a license because the drone's over a half a pound, and I passed the TRUST safety test." I don't mention that TRUST is impossible to fail. You do a multiple-choice questionnaire until you get it correct.

"Okay, then let's make this thing do its job."

We trace back a bit to a spot from where we can see where Hank went down. The crime scene tape is still there with new PENN STATE ANTHROPOLOGY signs. This early, without foot traffic, makes it feel as though we're the only people out here.

"Tell you what, Nate. If it's okay with you, I want to check out some of the spots farther out." I point to the rolling hills that ripple out from the creek. "Mach and I will look around while you take care of the photos. As you move the drone to the lookout point, come join us and we'll wrap it up."

"Works for me." His brow knits as he works. He's full concentration, sending out a vibe of confident competence.

"Thanks! Come on, boy." Mach doesn't hesitate to go with me, which makes me happy because Mach is so devoted to Nate. If Mach accepts me, it means Nate totally trusts me, too. And Mach knows it.

We take a lesser-worn dirt path through the woods. The land angles up and through the trees. I follow a tiny winding brook that in spring babbles over algae-coated rocks. The summer heat has dried much of the flow and the bright-green moss has long since turned to brown, except in patches that are protected by tree shade. I step onto a small foot-bridge spanning the widest part of the stream, and my shoulder almost pops out of its socket with a strong wrench-ing motion. I look back. Mach's standing stock-still, unsure of the bridge.

"Mach. Come on, doggie. I know your daddy's brought you this way before." I muster my most enthusiastic voice and try not to sound pushy. Mach is 110 pounds of canine that I can't force to do anything he doesn't want to. "Please?"

Mach ignores me, starts to sniff the ground. A nearby rustling startles us both, and without warning Mach leaps over the short span and chases after a flash of black and white. It's not a genetically modified squirrel, but a skunk. It quickly disappears from my view, but Mach's nose is locked on to its target.

"Maaaach!" His sudden movement yanks me forward, and I'm running as fast as I can before I belatedly let go of the leash.

Now you know how Hank may have felt.

Mach aims straight for a long log, shoving his snout into the end.

"No, Mach, come here, boy. Now!"

To my utter surprise, Mach stops, lifts his head, and looks at me, ears pricked.

"Come here, that's a good boy." Mach prances back to me, and I lean down and grab the leash. I pet him. "Good, good dog."

Only after we're back on the dirt path, not far from the lookout point, does the consequence of Mach's detour take effect. For whatever reason, the skunk withheld its spray until we were out of the area. Pure essence of skunk fills my nostrils, my mouth. I cough, and Mach stops, looks over his shoulder to where he left the skunk in its log.

"Don't even think about it, doggie." I keep my voice

stern and march forward as though I'm really in control of the situation. When in fact I suspect we're both going to need a round of antiskunk shampoo when we get home.

The *whirr* of the drone breaks through my thoughts as the clearing comes into sight.

"C'mon, boy." I'm anxious to reach the lookout. I'm also a little spooked, to be honest. Trinity didn't want me to come up here, and while I haven't seen anyone but Nate, and Mach, a killer would know how to hide.

Mach has other ideas. He's stopped again, and this time he's whining.

"What, Mach, is it the drone? It's your dad. He'll be here soon."

I do my best to tug Mach the remaining ten yards or so, through the last stretch of trees to the wide-open cliffside. I'm moving my feet through dead leaves as high as my ankles and trying to not think about the snakes and threat of Lyme disease from ticks that teem over this part of the country.

That's when the glint of the sun hits my vision. It's my turn to come to a dead stop, and thankfully Mach's agreeable. Because I've found something unusual.

Chapter Twenty-One

"WHAT IS IT, Mach?" I squat down to examine where I saw the flash of sunlight.

A small square piece of metal that reminds me of the brass belt buckles I spent years shining, first in Annapolis and later in the fleet. But it's not a uniform buckle. It's a lighter.

I palm the object, cold against my skin. It's finely ridged, and when I snap it open, it rewards me with a quick flame.

"Whoa!" I quickly snap it closed. The brush is dry and the threat of fire ever present.

Mach whines again and the drone hovers above us, then expertly lands on an even piece of ground. Footsteps sound and I turn to see Nate approach.

"That was a perfect landing, Captain."

"I got lucky. The camera is top notch and allowed me to see the tiniest details. Including whatever that shiny object is that you found." He stops in front of me and hands me my phone. "All the footage should be there for your viewing pleasure."

"Great!" I hold up the lighter. "Mach helped me find

this. It's pretty fancy. I'll put in on the Stonebridge social media site. Someone's sure to be looking for it." I slip the lighter into my pocket. "The lighter's not the only treasure we found. Mach chased—"

"A skunk. I know; I smelled it a quarter of a mile back. He has an affinity for anything fluffy and black with a white stripe." Nate shakes his head, a bemused grin lighting up his face as he looks at his beloved pooch. "You can't stay out of trouble, can you, Mach?"

Mach's huge tail thumps on the ground, his head cocked at an intelligent angle, as if he completely understands Nate. His front left paw is curved in a C, a classic Shiloh shepherd pose.

"He's such a smart dog, except for skunks. But it didn't spray you directly, did it, Mach? Not that it matters at this point." My eyes are still watering, and I can't imagine how bad we'd smell if Mach had taken a direct hit.

"I'll make sure to use his antiskunk shampoo on him when we get home. Outside, with the hose." He turns back to Mach. "You're not going inside until you get a bath, dude."

"I might need it, too." The skunk's essence surrounds us like a fog bank.

"Will you look at that." Nate walks to the edge of the overlook. It's a flat area of well-worn ground that ends at a cliff that's about twenty feet above the tree line. Nothing like the outcroppings that surround Stonebridge and populate the Appalachian Trail—those take hours to hike up to—but it's a nice place to catch your breath. When a skunk hasn't perfumed the area.

"Stunning." I take a couple steps to be right next to Nate. Mach sits to one side, as if he's observing the panoramic scenery, too. The lush green of the tree leaves contrast with the pale-cream sun-bleached grass that I was afraid of setting on fire. Birds flit from one side of the waterway, flashes of white, blue, black. The creek spans approximately one football field's length, but with the trees and over brush it appears far narrower.

"I don't see how a shooter could have seen Hank, or my mother, from here."

"Ye of little faith." Nate pulls a tiny pair of binoculars from his backpack.

"I thought you only carried water and treats for Mach in that."

He waggles his brow. "You have no idea what secrets I keep, Angel."

"Give me a break." I reach for the binoculars, and quickly narrow in on the end of the left side of the weir. Sure enough, the flash of yellow crime scene tape appears.

"See it?" Nate asks.

"I do." I hand back the binoculars. "So all the killer needed was a good scope on their rifle," I think aloud.

"Pretty much." Nate sits on the ground and beckons for me to join him. "Let's enjoy this for a few minutes. Before the day makes us both too busy to relax."

I sit next to him and Mach moves to lie beside me.

Nate's arm curves around my waist, and he pulls me closer. "This is my idea of heaven."

"I couldn't agree—"

"I've got my girl and my dog and all the fresh air a man could ask for."

I giggle, as I'm certain was Nate's intention. "By *fresh air* do you mean eau du skunk?"

"*Wahooo.*" Mach gives one of his most unwolflike howls, triggering us both into belly laughter. Nate's right. This is heaven, right here in Stonebridge, Pennsylvania.

Except there's a killer at large, and we're sitting on the same spot he may have shot Hank from.

THE REST OF the morning involves scrubbing myself free of skunk smell and deciding to work outside at a café table in front of Latte Love. Working in my retail area isn't a great idea as it's a small, closed space where my customers might detect any lingering skunk scent. Fortunately it's not raining, I'm under an umbrella, and it's time for me to order stock again, so all I need is my laptop.

Trinity agreed to meet me here instead of in the store for our usual coffee catch-up. This meeting has more urgency with two shootings still unsolved. Still, we enjoy our cappuccinos, my second of the morning.

"I really wish you hadn't gone to Jacob's Run this morning, Angel," Trinity says. "At least you had Nate and his beast with you." She wrinkles her nose. I know I smell to high skunk heaven, even after taking two showers with the special shampoo that's supposed to neutralize skunk odor. It's much better than it was when I first came home—Ralph stopped calling for me, that's how bad it was—but Ava and Lily confirmed that I'm carrying around leftover stench.

"We didn't go anywhere near the crime scene. There wasn't a crowd on the path, either. Probably because you've shut down the creek."

"At least folks are abiding the restriction. Thanks for talking this out in person, Angel. I know I'm being grouchy. I'm at the point in the investigation where we have to figure it out before another shot is fired, yet nothing's breaking. I can't help but think there's an important detail I've overlooked." Trinity's gaze is obscured by her sunglasses, but the downward curve of her mouth conveys her frustration.

"You, miss a detail? No way. More like this case isn't straightforward. Which reminds me, do you know anything about Hank Price having gambling debts?" At her hesitation, I go on. "Verity told me and Eloise that almost all of her money is gone, and she believes it's because Hank fell off the wagon. He's a gambling addict. Was."

"Yes, she told me that, but not right away. It took two trips out to her place to dig it out of her. Verity is like an onion, that's for sure. My team has done every kind of digging, from the local casino to illegal online gambling that we're aware of. There's no evidence that Hank Price had been gambling."

"But we're certain he moved a large amount recently, right?" I ask.

"Yes. We've checked the bank accounts and investments, so we know he withdrew large amounts of cash, frequently, with the largest only days before his murder. Because it's cash, though, it's impossible to trace it to the recipient."

"None of this makes any sense. Two shots, from opposite sides of the river. One kills Hank, the other grazes my mom. One's intentional by all appearances. The other seems too coincidental to not be related, but could it have been an anomaly? Someone goofing around?" I ask.

"Highly doubtful. But yes, it's possible. Your mother's shooter could have been a copycat, some jerk getting a thrill from aiming at the same place Hank's murder occurred. It wouldn't be the first time something that bizarre has happened. You know that, Ms. All-Night-Cold-Case-TV-Binge-Viewer."

"I do," I admit.

Trinity sighs and looks at her phone. I know she has to get back to work. But I need more answers. Like her, I'm frustrated.

"Do you think Verity's telling us the truth about everything? I keep getting the feeling that she's not being completely up front."

"And I keep telling you that your theory that Verity is the killer is pure speculation, Angel. You asked me to trust you, which I do. Trust me on this. Murders get solved by facts more than intuition." Trinity stands and throws her paper cup in the street side recycling receptacle. "If you can figure out what she's hiding, it might lead us to where the money's gone. If we can find out who's been getting all that cash, we'll have our suspect."

"But why kill Hank if he's been a cash cow?"

Trinity shrugs. "I don't know. It's possible they knew that Hank was getting to the bottom of the barrel and didn't need him anymore." Trinity's explanation resembles the speculation she's accused me of making. I stay quiet on this, though. I'm not risking being kicked off the all-volunteer investigator team bench.

"Okay. I'm going to take a look at the drone footage later. I'll let you know if anything pops out at me."

"Sounds good. I'll talk to you later," she says.

"Bye."

Trinity gets into her unmarked vehicle and pulls away from the curb.

I try to refocus on inventory orders but I know I'm wasting my time, so I click open the drone app, also installed on my computer. Nate's done a great job at capturing what I wanted to look at. The weir, both sides of Jacob's Run, the various spots where a shooter might have crouched—waiting to get Hank or my mother in their sight—flash across my screen.

The outside lighting isn't ideal, but I can make out enough detail on the video. I have my back to the building, and I'm the only one out here as several patrons recently departed. Kevin's bussing tables and I notice a broom leaning against a chair. Nate did well when he hired the widower. His attention to detail makes me wonder if he ever served in the military, but now isn't the time for chitchat. Not when my insides are driving me to solve this case.

My attention back on the video, I play and replay various drone shots. Heat roils in my gut at the reminder that someone deliberately shot at Mom. I focus in on where I stood with Nate and Mach earlier, the area where I found the lighter.

Dang it! I forgot to mention the lighter to Trinity. I don't think it's more than a hiker's personal item that fell out of a pocket, but what was I just thinking about attention to detail?

I look at the area Trinity said Hank's bullet came from, as confirmed by ballistics. It's hard to see much of the ground as there are far more trees on that side of the creek. My gaze catches on something that's out of place, though. I freeze the video, zoom in. Right at the farthest spot where the killer would have stood and been able to hit Hank. There's a small shelf of sorts under where the ground rises above the creek. It looks like a rock outcropping, but smaller than the ones I've hiked miles through the woods to—and sat on for hours—to watch hawks circle at eye level. I zoom in as close as I can.

There, amid pale grass growing through rock cracks, is a dark circle. Some kind of debris lay next to it, and if I'm not mistaken, it looks an awful lot like an exploded firework.

Bryce and I heard a firework when we were on the water, right before we found Hank. On the day Mom was shot, she and the research assistant didn't hear a firework, but they thought they heard a gunshot. I found the lighter on the side Hank's shooter had fired from. Did the killer not realize until too late that they didn't have their lighter available to ignite a firework when it came time to fire at Mom?

It takes me several minutes to confirm that there's no evidence of a firework on the creek bank from where Mom's shooter stood.

My hand's shaking as I grab my phone.

"Miss me already?" Trinity asks.

"Tell me something, did your team find any fireworks when they scoured the crime scene?"

"We did, but nothing that had been fired recently."

"I think I found something." I tell her my suspicions, and relay my lighter theory.

"That sounds too good to be true, but let's go with it. Where's the lighter now?"

"In my shorts, at home." In the laundry bin. I'd been so intent on getting rid of my skunk stank that I forgot about the lighter.

"Did you touch it?"

"With bare hands. I'm sorry, I'm certain my prints are all over it. I never thought about it being evidence until now." I feel like such a rookie.

"I have to take care of some things, and then I'll be by to pick it up." To her credit, Trinity's tone is neutral. If I were her, I'd be ticked at my stupidity.

"Thanks." I disconnect the call, staring at my screen. *What am I missing?*

The café table moves under my laptop, a wrought iron leg hits my knee.

"Ow!"

"I'm so sorry, Angel. I guess I'm still getting used to this big broom." Kevin offers an apologetic smile, his gaze on my hands gripping my laptop. "Your computer okay?"

"Yes, yes, it's fine."

"Kevin, we need you at the counter." Amy, the worker that Nate and I each employ, speaks from the wide granite front steps.

"I'll be right there," Kevin replies, his gaze never leaving mine. I must look and smell a sight. I didn't bother slapping on any makeup after my shower, and left my hair unstyled. I figured I'd be rewashing it later.

"Hi, Amy," I greet her, and she replies with a quick wave before disappearing back into Latte Love.

I stand and start throwing my stuff into my Belgian tapestry tote that has Vermeer's painting known as *Girl with a Pearl Earring* woven into it. It's one of my shop's top sellers. I'm all about marketing my wares whenever possible.

"Are you finished?" Kevin points at my mug. Unlike Trinity, I prefer using the Latte Love blue-speckled ceramic mugs when I'm not doing takeaway.

"I am, thank you." I'm itching to take off down the street, to my building, to the lighter. But seeing Kevin reminds me of what I discovered in the library.

"Kevin, I'm sorry I never knew Mabel."

His eyes widen, and his breath catches. *Crap.* I've triggered his grief, no doubt. Sometimes I'm not the most tactful. Kevin's silence compels me to continue.

"I don't mean to overstep. Let me start over. I heard that you wanted an hourly job because you're trying to keep busy. I want you to know that I totally get it. I lost my husband six years ago and it's really tough, those first couple of years. I was at the library the other day and saw the plaque for Mabel. She was really loved."

He nods, his composure back. And is that relief on his face? I remember how comforting it was to talk to someone who understood my loss.

"Yes, Mabel was a big part of the community. If only she hadn't had her disability, she might still be here. I'm grateful for every minute I had with her. I wish it could have been eighty years instead of the forty that we were married."

"Again, sorry that I've mentioned something so painful. I

tend to put my foot in my mouth."

"No, you're very kind. I appreciate that you said anything. I take it that you and the boss are an item?"

"Ah, yes, we are." I smile, see the subject changer for what it is. I want to tell him that he'll have his happy times again, but I've said enough. He was married twice as long as Tom and me. It's going to take him a while to even begin to think about being happy without her. "I'll see you soon, I'm sure."

"You will." He goes inside and I strike off for my store, my brain firing on all investigative synapses. My gut's telling me that I'm close, maybe that Trinity and I have already solved the murder.

We just have to figure out who did it.

Chapter Twenty-Two

TRINITY MADE IT clear she's not in a hurry to pick up the lighter, which gives me time to see for myself if I've missed any clue it may offer.

Using the full-spectrum lighted magnifying glass that's attached to my office desk, I examine the lighter from every angle. I see a trademark, and immediately do an internet search. Interesting. The make and particular model of this lighter places its manufacture anywhere between 1980 and 1984. Which makes sense, as it's old and worn. Without the magnifier, I wouldn't have been able to make out the engraving, much less the manufacturer.

To KM
From MS
You're the light of my life

I have no idea who KM and MS are. So much for solving the murder, or even my mother's shooting.

"Is it true you stopped by without coming into my office?" My stomach does a warm flip at the familiar voice. Nate's standing in front of my desk.

"Whoa, I never heard you come in." The shop's busy with customers is probably why. It's all white noise to me when I'm focused.

"Sorry, I didn't mean to frighten you. I come bearing a gift." He places an iced coffee on a coaster next to my Vermeer tote bag. I was so anxious to get to the lighter, I haven't moved it from where I dropped it.

"Thank you. I already had two cappuccinos while I worked outside Latte Love. Trinity and I put our heads together but so far we're still stumped. By the way, I had a nice conversation with Kevin. He's quite the worker."

"Yeah, I lucked out the day Kevin Moore applied for a job slinging coffee." Nate visibly inhales, raises his brow. "It's a good thing you spent a couple of hours working outside, because you still smell like skunk." He smiles. "Better not go out front. You'll scare away your customers. Did you use the shampoo I gave you?"

"I did. Why do you smell so much cleaner than I do?" I ask.

"I don't. Your sniffer's just numb from too much skunk is all."

"Plus you have the coffee-bean scent to cover your stinkiness." The aroma of roasting beans is the reason I always enjoy walking into Latte Love whenever Nate's roasting.

"I do have the coffee shield, you're right." He walks around the desk and starts massaging my shoulders. "You are tighter than Mach's leash when I try to get him in water.

What can I do to help?"

"Lots of things come to mind." I use a sultry tone.

He chuckles, then his fingers still. "Have you figured out who the lighter might belong to?"

"No. Here, look." I invite him to peer through the magnifying lens.

"Huh. KM and MS," he says.

I tell him how old it is, and the manufacturer. "It was a common sweetheart gift back in the day. Sold in local jewelry—"

"Stores," he finishes for me. "Like the one right here in Stonebridge?"

"Nate, you're a gem." I blush. "Sorry, very bad pun. I never even thought to ask Lilibeth Draper. Do you think it could be from her shop? Even if it is, what are the odds she'd keep receipts going back that far?"

"There's only one way to find out."

NATE HAS TO get back to Latte Love but we walk together down Main Street, and kiss good-bye in front of the brick building, with a promise to have grilled chicken kebabs tonight. It's both Nate's and the twins' favorite dish of mine. I keep going two more blocks until I stop and enter Draper's Diamonds and Pearls.

"Angel! Are you finally treating yourself to something

nice?" Lilibeth Draper stands behind the counter, her dark hair shimmering with indigo highlights. The store she inherited from her grandfather is in an historical building, like so many of Stonebridge's businesses. There's nothing historical about her retail area, though. Spanking-clean glass display cases show off her hand-selected jewelry collection. Everything from precious gems and pearls to high-end synthetic stones fill the cases. An exquisite crystal vase filled with fresh-cut local wildflowers graces the end of her counter. I smile at Crystal's obvious touch; my sister supplies many of the local shops with flowers.

"Hi, Lilibeth. The girls both love the earrings you helped me pick out last Christmas. I don't think either of them have taken them off since." I purchased matching sets of drop earrings for them in their respective school colors. Ruby for Ava and sapphire for Lily.

"Good to know." Her eyes narrow on the lighter as I place it on the glass top. "What's this treasure?"

"Do you recognize it? I found it on the Jacob's Run hiking path. Sorry but I have to keep it in the plastic bag."

"Okay. I sure do recognize this." She picks up the plastic bag and peers at the lighter through the plastic. "Both my grandad and father sold this particular lighter for a span of ten to fifteen years. We get folks coming in every now and then asking for an appraisal." She smiles. "They're usually engraved, and have high sentimental value. Sadly, I can't buy them back for resale. They're not at all profitable. But it's a good, sturdy lighter, and probably still works. Have you tried it?" She places it back on the counter and slides it toward me.

"I'm not here to sell it. I'm wondering if there's any chance you have records of purchases that far back? There's an engraving."

"We don't keep anything longer than a few years, not unless they're high-value items."

Disappointment clenches my stomach tight, and I chew on my lower lip.

"Have you checked for an engraving?" Lilibeth offers.

"Yes, but I have no idea who it is. And I lived away from Stonebridge for years. My memory of longtime local families has faded, unfortunately."

"I'm sorry. The town hall visitors' center has a lost and found box. If someone local dropped this lighter, they'll be looking for it. What was the engraving?"

I tell her. "MS and KM could be any two lovebirds, am I right?"

She laughs. "For sure."

"Thank you for your time, Lilibeth." I turn toward the door.

"Anytime."

I exit into the bright afternoon sunshine and head back to my shop. I'll get the car and drive the lighter over to the police station before I go back to my inventory. I'm not having any luck with the murder solving today.

As I pass Latte Love, I see Kevin back out on the sidewalk, this time wiping down the empty bistro tables. Several are occupied, which makes me happy for Nate. He's a brilliant businessman.

"Hi again, Kevin."

"Angel." He nods, keeps cleaning tables. As I pass, I think of Nate's reply when I told him what a good employee Kevin is.

Yeah, I lucked out when I hired Kevin Moore.

Kevin Moore. KM.

But the engraving was MS, not MM. My mind flashes to the memorial plaque in the library. MABEL SMITH MOORE.

The lighter is Kevin's. I stop on the sidewalk, meaning to turn back toward Latte Love. If it's his lighter…

But what if it's the shooter's? Facts, snippets of the investigation, recalled conversations all vie for my mind's spotlight.

Mabel could still be here…

Hank practiced for only a short time…

My suspicion that Verity has been holding back something related to the murder rears at the same time.

There's only one person who has the answer.

"ANGEL! COME ON in. Let me guess, my lantern is here?" Verity opens her front door wide. Moose is at her side, his tail wagging faster than my windshield wipers during a summer thunderstorm.

"No, but you'll have it later today. I've verified that the driver has your address. How are you, Verity?" I can't help myself from asking. She looks paler than in the restaurant, if that's possible. The strain of the past week seems to have aged her a decade. Moose licks my hand, accepts my robust hug. He's a sweet dog who has lost his loved one, too.

"Awful." She turns and heads toward a large, open living room. I stand up from loving on Moose.

"Please sit down. I really appreciate you stopping by. I haven't had a chance to look at my financial figures again. Maybe we could work on them next week? They've released the body. I'm thinking the middle of next week for the service." She's babbling and I wish I didn't have to confront her while she's like this. Her eyes are glazed, and it throws me back to how empty I was after Tom died.

I sit on the edge of what has to be the brightest floral-print sofa in Stonebridge. The space is liberally decorated with several items from Shop 'Round the World, a testament to what a loyal customer she's been.

But not a truthful widow.

"Verity, I didn't come here to work on your cashflow issue. I have a question to ask and I need a straight answer from you," I say.

She blinks away a layer of the shell-shocked appearance. "Sure, whatever." Her body tenses as if...as if I'm about to deliver a killing blow.

"Why didn't Hank practice as a chiropractor? Or, more to the point, what made him stop? The truth, Verity."

Does she realize that her answer is a matter of life or death?

Chapter Twenty-Three

VERITY STARES AT me for a long moment, unmoving. The silence is broken only by Moose most unselfconsciously licking himself. He lies on a miniature loveseat turned dog bed that's upholstered to match the one I'm sitting on.

"Well?" I ask.

She expels her breath, sets her hands on her knees.

"Hank was accused of hurting a patient, right after we married. We'd just set up the practice together. I'd been working with another doctor in Harrisburg. It was going to be our practice, Stonebridge's single stop for the best chiropractic care. When Hank's patient said he'd disabled her, we thought we'd lose it all. The patient threatened a malpractice suit. Hank swore up and down that she'd already been disabled, that his adjustment couldn't have possibly hurt her further. But if we'd been sued…"

"You would have had to shut down both of your practices."

She nods. Her knuckles are snow white against her tanned skin. "I would have been guilty by association. The husband approached us with a deal. He'd keep it quiet, no lawyers involved, for a settlement. We didn't have a settlement to give him, so we agreed to a permanent monthly payment. As long as the woman lived."

"And after she died?"

"That was it. The payments were supposed to stop."

"Did they?"

Verity shoots me a furtive glance. She thinks I've figured it all out. I'm close, but I need her to fill in the missing piece.

"I thought they had. I mean, they did. When she passed, Hank told me that we were finally free of that noose around our neck. But then the husband asked for more money. Said he'd had to caretake for so long that he'd missed out on job opportunities. He'd been a janitor for the school system, retired after forty years. He has a pension, for heaven's sake. Why he wanted more from Hank was nothing more than greed, if you ask me."

"Who are we talking about, Verity?" I know, or at least am 99 percent certain, but I need her to say it.

"Kevin Moore. His wife, Mabel, was Hank's patient, a sweet woman by all accounts." Verity sniffs, wipes her nose with a tissue she took from her pocket. "But I never could see her, or her husband, as more than the extortionists they were."

"Why didn't you or Hank go to the police?"

"I begged him to, or to at least consult a lawyer. Appearances meant everything to Hank. I grew up in a similar home. Hank believed that the minute the Moores' claim became public, we'd lose our licenses. I was doing well and had a solid base of patients. The business grew exponentially those first few years of our marriage. Paying the Moores off was the right decision, I'm certain."

"Until Kevin wanted money after Mabel died?" I ask. Verity's countenance has remarkably lightened. She's unburdening a decade's worth of extortion and lies.

And handed me Hank's murderer on a platter.

"I didn't know about that part, not until after Hank was killed. When I realized the money was missing. And I know what you're getting at. But can we be so certain it was Kevin Moore who killed Hank? It makes sense that he was angry at Hank. But I never thought it was enough to kill Hank, or I would have told the police." Her gaze is on a distant, unseen spot as she recalls what happened.

"Hank and Kevin had an altercation about a month after Mabel died. Kevin showed up here, and when Hank saw him on the video doorbell, he told me to lock myself in the basement storage room and call the police if it got too heated. But I stayed on the stairs, with the door cracked. I heard everything." She begins to sob. There's a clock on the fireplace mantel that chimes the hour. Six o'clock. I was supposed to be home for dinner by now, but it has to wait. Nate and the girls will understand. Maybe. Ralph, not so much.

I need answers so I stay put. I'll wait as long as I need to, so that I can give Trinity the full story this time.

It's smarter to give Verity space so that she doesn't leave out details, but my patience is growing thin. So is Moose's. He's stopped cleaning his privates and is pacing near French doors that open to a ginormous paved patio.

Verity clears her throat. "Kevin Moore had so much venom in his voice when he spoke to Hank. He told him that it wasn't fair that Hank had ruined his life, and Mabel's." Verity looks at me. "Don't you think it's telling, that he put himself before Mabel? As if he'd suffered. He wasn't in a chair. He didn't need crutches. Anyway, he went on and on about how it wasn't fair that Hank and I were able to live such a wonderful life, enjoy community esteem, while he and Mabel could never have the life they deserved. I prayed that Hank would tell him off, finally. Tell him that he didn't hurt Mabel. The woman was dead, why hold back? But Hank didn't say anything. He was too caring in that way. Kevin told Hank that we'd be hearing from him. That was two months before Hank was shot. After Kevin confronted Hank, we assumed we'd be hit with a lawsuit, but it never came. Hank died before it ever happened." Her voice cracks.

"Why do you think Kevin never outright sued? It would have awarded a lump sum he could have counted on. Hank could have changed his mind about the payments and cut Kevin off."

"Kevin didn't sue because he knew that the proof that Hank didn't hurt Mabel would come out! Hank had such low self-esteem he was willing to believe he'd injured her. But I found something in Hank's files today, something Hank found two days before he was killed." Verity stands and starts to walk away from the living room to what I can see is an office. "Let me get it. It's in the office." She disappears beyond the entry.

"*Woof!*" Moose's bark echoes across the room, followed by a menacing growl. I look over and see the hairs on his nape are spiked straight up.

Kevin Moore stands on the patio, pointing a rifle through the French door window. The barrel is aimed right between my eyes.

"Um, Verity? You might want to call 9-1-1."

"WHERE IS SHE?" Kevin Moore's face is full of thunderous rage as he screams from the other side of the door, a far cry from his congenial barista persona. "I will kill you, Angel! Open the door or I'll shoot it open!" he shouts.

Moose is growling and barking and scratching at the door as if it's Kevin, and I've no doubt the dog would fight until Kevin shot him.

"Don't point that rifle at me, Kevin! Let me crate the dog!" I shout. Not so much for his benefit but for Verity's. She hasn't come back out here or answered me, so I'm hoping—*please, God*—she's doing the same thing she did when Hank had his last conversation with Kevin. I hold my bare hands up, praying that Kevin takes the bait. That he believes I'm no threat to a man holding a lethal weapon.

"Hurry up." He spits the words as he motions with the tip of the rifle. Not the kind of firearm etiquette I like to see, but all I care about is buying time.

I look around the room for a crate as Moose keeps up his best devil dog snarling. *There it is!* His crate looks more like a regular end table instead of Mach's budget-friendlier plastic one.

"Come on, Moose." I grasp his collar and of course he totally ignores me, clawing at the hardwood floor for purchase. I'm not a weakling by any means, but he's solid muscle and intent on protecting his domain.

"Get him away or I'll take care of it." Kevin lowers the rifle barrel to the level of Moose's snout.

I freeze. Not from fright, or because trying to move Moose away from the door is proving impossible. Kevin can shout at me, bully me, point a weapon at me.

Nobody threatens an innocent family pet on my watch.

"You'll have to shoot through me first." I stand in between Moose and the French door. Moose immediately shoves his nose between my legs in an effort to reach the window, throwing my chest and hands against the glass. If Kevin fires now, I'll be with Tom, this time forever.

Startled, Kevin takes a fast step back, then another. His foot catches on...the small Japanese lantern I gave to Verity the other day. She moved it to the patio, next to a planter filled with lavender.

I watch as Kevin falls backward, landing butt first. His torso and head follow, but he's still conscious, scuttling with his rifle and the patio pavers to get back on his feet.

"Police!"

Trinity stands up from behind the low wall that surrounds the patio. She's wearing a Kevlar vest, weapon drawn. Several officers appear, closing their circle around Kevin, all firearms pointed at him.

"Is it safe to come out?" Verity asks at the edge of the living room. Moose runs to his mistress, and she squats down to hug him.

I look back outside. Kevin's on his stomach while an officer cuffs him. Trinity sees me and mouths "Okay?"

"We're good." I flash my bestie a thumbs-up before turning back to Verity and Moose.

"Yes, it's safe. You're safe. It's all over now, Verity."

Chapter Twenty-Four

"INTERESTING. YOU'RE SAYING I was shot at in an effort to deflect the police from the real killer?" Mom asks from her seat at my dining room table. Mom and Dad, Trinity, Tony the professor, the twins, Nate, and I have polished off an entire platter of pineapple chicken kebabs, a summertime favorite around here. Trinity agreed to do our unofficial debrief of the investigation here, and I'm so glad I offered my place. There's nothing more satisfying to me than feeding a hungry family, and sharing around the table.

Solving a murder comes in close, though. This could be habit forming. It's a good thing murder is so rare in Stonebridge.

Trinity nods. "Kevin Moore has admitted to firing both shots. He killed Hank out of unspeakable rage triggered by his grief over Mabel's death. The idea to shoot Livvie came to him when he realized he had more than one person trying to figure out it was him." She flashes a bright smile, and I return it.

"It makes sense to me that Kevin wanted everyone to think the weir's discovery and possibility of becoming an archaeological treasure was the motive." Tony's face is the picture of adoration as he speaks, his gaze never leaving Trinity.

"Thank goodness he didn't hurt anyone else," Mom says.

"I told you I thought working on the weir project might stir up trouble," Dad says from his seat next to Mom. He has his arm around her shoulders, and I've noticed a lot more affection between them. Turns out being shot has an upside, not to minimize the sheer terror Mom went through.

"How close are you to figuring out the weir's age, Tony?" Ava pipes in.

"That's Professor Tony to you." Lily can't help herself.

Tony laughs. "Everyone at this table has earned a first-name basis with each other, I'd say." He focuses on Ava. "I'm no closer than I was a week ago. But I'm no further, either. My team has the rest of the summer to work on it."

Trinity's smile is so wide, I swear her face is going to split. Happiness wells deep in my chest, right at my heart chakra, as Eloise would describe. It's the best to see my bestie finding love again. No one deserves it more.

"The one thing I don't understand is why Verity held back from telling the police about Kevin sooner." Nate's absentmindedly stroking Mach's head, which is even with my shoulder as the pooch sits between us.

"Love," I reply. All eyes are on me. "Verity loved Hank, and knew the sacrifices he'd made for her success. She was unable to see that Kevin could have murdered Hank, if you ask me."

"Denial isn't a river and all that?" Nate asks.

"Exactly. She was telling the truth about Hank's gambling addiction, from which he recovered, by the way. But it's important to remember that any kind of addiction affects the whole family. Verity loved Hank and by association was capable of deep levels of denial where his behavior was concerned. It's why she didn't notice the missing money. She didn't want to."

"Kevin knew Hank was down to his last, money-wise," Trinity adds. "It's what led him to kill him. Hank represented everything wrong with Kevin's life, as far as Kevin was concerned. And before you all think I'm insightful like Angel, stop. This all came out during Kevin's confession."

"Is the DA going to press charges on Verity for impeding an investigation?"

Trinity shakes her head. "Probably not. Verity's behavior this last week falls under the umbrella of shock and grief, to be fair."

"I can't believe I hired a killer barista," Nate says.

"Correction: you hired a killer. You're the only killer barista in Stonebridge," I say.

"I'm glad you caught the murderer, Trinity," Mom says. "Now we can go full steam ahead on the weir with no worries!"

Dad rolls his eyes, the girls giggle, and Nate squeezes my hand. I turn to him and give him a quick kiss. "Want to go—"

"Up on the roof? Always." Nate smiles.

"Actually, I'm thinking of something with a better view. What are you doing tomorrow morning?"

"THIS IS THE best date you've come up with yet." Nate's voice is in my ear, which is covered with a headphone. He's next to me in the Cessna as I bank over the east side of Stonebridge and fly us along Jacob's Run. The waterway is a ribbon of blues and greens with yellow stretches here and there. It's easy to think nothing bad ever happened down there, that the only mystery is how old the V-shaped rock formation, visible through the shimmering water, is.

"Yeah, well, one of us has to keep things fresh," I say.

"I can show you fresh, my Angel." His reply bursts with promise. Affection. That four-letter word, too.

My laughter goes from all-out to dead silent. "Did you just say 'my' Angel?" It takes me a second to realize the pounding in my ears is my heart. Nate's not the type to tease about anything serious. He's also not the type of guy who lays claim to a woman like she's a piece of property.

"I did. I love you, Angel."

Nate's eyes are full of sunshine, hope, and my future.

"I love you, too."

A quick kiss is all we're going to enjoy until I land at the tiny regional airport on the other side of Stonebridge. The plane hits a patch of turbulence, making it dip and rise roller-coaster style. I don't fight it, as *chasing the aircraft*—a naval aviation term—never works. I can feel Nate's gaze on me the entire time. I glance over at him expecting to see his eyes glittering with love, or at least lust, but instead they reflect…terror. His skin is pale and his knuckles white, gripping his armrest.

"What's wrong? Are you prone to motion sickness?" I ask.

"I'm not a big fan of flying. I should have told you." He speaks through clenched teeth.

Poor Nate! Why didn't I ask him? Just because he was a ship driver doesn't mean he's a fan of flying. Flight has never made me sick, but I've had some green-gilled days aboard ship.

"It's okay, Nate. It's just a little turbulence is all. It'll pass."

"There's no such thing as a 'little' turbulence around you, Angel Warren."

The End

Want more? Don't miss Angel's next adventure in
A Wasp in the Woods!

Join Tule Publishing's newsletter for more great reads and weekly deals!

Acknowledgements

With heartfelt gratitude to the entire Tule team. Jane, Meghan, Sinclair and Nikki: you rock. Thank you to the most unwelcome bald faced wasp nest that I and my hedge trimmers happened upon this past summer. There lurks a book in every life experience! Many thanks to Hope Stephan and Heidi Hormel for helping with last-minute tweaks. Most of all, thank you dear readers for supporting my writing journey and letting me know how much you enjoy my stories. We are in this together!

If you enjoyed *A Mid-Summer Murder*,
you'll love the next book in the…

Shop 'Round the World series

Book 1: *A Santa Stabbing*

Book 2: *A Mid-Summer Murder*

Book 3: *A Wasp in the Woods*
Coming in August 2023

Available now at your favorite online retailer!

About the Author

Geri Krotow is the bestselling author of over 25 novels of romantic suspense, contemporary romance and women's fiction. A US Naval Academy graduate and Navy veteran, Geri's strong heroines are reader favorites. Geri's Shop 'Round the World series with Tule is her cozy mystery debut.

Thank you for reading

A Mid-Summer Murder

If you enjoyed this book, you can find more from all our great authors at TulePublishing.com, or from your favorite online retailer.

TULE
PUBLISHING